Insinuations

Barbara Winkes

ISBN: 978-1-0690835-6-2

Cover art © May Dawney Designs

Created with Atticus

For D.

Chapter One

J ordan braced herself for the inevitable question. When it came, she was ready.

"Do you want to see Pratt today?" her partner Derek Henderson asked. TJ Pratt had once done time with Phil Hobbs, a wanted felon high on their list. He was also a longtime friend of Jordan's birthparents whom she hadn't seen in almost twenty years. She had good enough reasons to stall this visit, and even one that would convince Derek.

"He's not going anywhere. After baby girl threw up on me earlier, I'd rather go home and shower, start fresh tomorrow."

Derek, oblivious, nodded. "I'll see you later?"

Jordan would have preferred to spend the evening curled up on her couch, but one of their colleagues was having his retirement party at the *Code 7* this evening. She had to make an appearance at least.

"Sure. I won't be long though. We'll check on Pratt first thing tomorrow."

"All right, see you there."

"Yeah."

Jordan took the elevator down to the lobby, breathing a sigh of relief when the sliding doors of the department closed behind her, and she could escape the looks and whispers behind her back. In her car, she regarded herself critically in the mirror.

They had rescued the baby from a volatile domestic abuse situation. The mother was barely conscious and transported to the hospital. It was unclear whether she would make it. The officers first on the scene had made a judgment call and notified the detectives.

They had been waiting for social services to arrive. The uniformed cop first on the scene had with unmistakable certainty found the woman with the least maternal instincts, when he handed the little girl to Jordan. She was cute. Jordan felt for her. However, she realized she was not capable of consoling a crying baby or handling being thrown up on. Her shirt might have to go in the trash. She felt like crying, angry at herself because of it, and all of it had little to do with the stained clothing. Jordan hated crying, always had.

It was good to be back at work though. It was what she needed. After all, she had a house to pay for. She had gotten a good deal, the fact that the man who had sold it to her was a serial killer, notwithstanding. She had a job and a roof over her head. Most importantly, she was alive, and so were Lori Gleason and Judy Lawrence. Others had not been so lucky. She had to remember that.

Walking up the stairs to her porch, Jordan was once again fascinated by how much this place felt like hers, like home. Her mind had blocked out the first visits with the realtor or when she went to see him at his place and discovered a secret door leading to his torture chamber.

There were no ghosts in this house. It was her safe space, ironically. Jordan went straight to the bathroom where she stripped and tossed the shirt in the sink. She'd give it one more chance. She stepped into the shower stall, washing off the grime of the day in quick, brisk moves. While naked and vulnerable, she had to keep her mind blank, not have it invaded by flashes of the basement—or other, almost as disturbing memories that were bubbling closer to the surface lately.

Chances were Pratt wouldn't remember her. She'd do her job, question him regarding Hobbs, move on. It wasn't the universe conspiring against her that this happened now. Shit happened to good people, or those who tried to be. Wrapping the towel tightly around her, she sat on the rim of the tub, leaning forward.

Whether or not Jordan belonged into the category of good people wasn't always clear to her—she had cheated on her girl-friend, not once, but twice. She had left another woman with many question marks. She owed her some answers, sometime soon.

Get up. Get dressed. Go to the damn party. She couldn't bring herself to move. What if Pratt did remember her? Her picture had been all over the news. For all she knew, he was still hanging out with Jim and Kathryn Larson, worse, they might be around. She could perhaps get away with asking Derek to take care of Pratt, but she didn't want him or anyone, for that matter, to think she couldn't do the job. If she wanted special treatment, she'd need to give an explanation. Whether they'd go for the obvious one, or open a whole other can of worms, it would be bad for her in any case. Better to suffer through one morning of traveling back to a time she had long left behind.

Determined, Jordan put on clothes and dried her hair, willing herself to make it to tomorrow night. A couple of days off would do her some good, and maybe by then, Phil Hobbs would be back behind bars.

One of the best and most unpractical features of her new home was that it was a half-hour drive, twenty minutes on a good day, to the city center. She enjoyed the more remote, suburban living, but it wasn't close to work or any of the places her colleagues liked to hang out at the end of a shift. On the plus side, she might manage not to drink. The alternative was to spend an outrageous amount on cab fees. Jordan wasn't yet sure which one it would be.

She could hear the voices, talk and laughter, from the outside, momentarily overwhelmed by the impulse to flee. It was ridiculous. In there were people who had worked hard to save her life. To gossip about her was the last thing on their minds, especially not when Marcus, the retiree, paid for the drinks tonight. Jordan walked inside, immediately scanning the room for Derek. He sat at the bar with another homicide detective, a recent addition to the department. Her eyes fell on another table in the corner, occupied by a group of rookies, third year, almost fourth. Jordan knew most of them by name as she had worked with them on one case or another, Kate, Jensen, Libby and...

Ellie.

Her back was turned to Jordan, so she hadn't seen her coming in. Her hair was still blonde. Jordan smiled, remembering when Ellie had confessed she'd dyed it because of her ex's preferences. She missed her, but some of the reasons why she'd broken up with her in the first place were still valid, and even more so than before. When they first met, Jordan had struggled with a separation that could turn ugly at any point—which was mostly her own fault—now she struggled to keep her life together, day by day. It was the kinder solution not to involve another person in the chaos. At this moment, Ellie turned in her chair, and their eyes met.

Seconds ticked by before Ellie gave her a hesitant smile and then directed her attention back to her friends. Jordan had seen something else reflected in her gaze, the same longing that she felt, but couldn't give in to, not yet. It was better this way, if painful, but they both knew a thing or two about how to handle pain.

"Hey, Jordan! It's good to see you. I'm glad you made it." *Especially since I almost ended up dead*, she added what she suspected most of her co-workers of thinking these days, even though they wouldn't say it out loud. She had to stop it. It wasn't like she could read their minds, and she shouldn't try.

The brief touch to her shoulder made her wince with the expected phantom pain. Her body had healed, and she'd been off the meds for a while, but her mind still played tricks on her sometimes.

"Congrats, Marcus," she said. "You made it out of the madhouse on time."

There it was, the concerned expression people wore in her presence these days. "How are you doing?" he asked.

"I'm doing *fine*," she stressed.

"Well, I'm glad to hear that." Jordan spun around at the sound of a familiar voice, and all of a sudden, she was far from fine. Talk about her mind playing tricks on her. The image of the woman standing in front of her, smiling ruefully, didn't waver.

"I'll leave you two to it," Marcus said. "Enjoy the party."

Bethany waited until he had left to talk to a couple of other guests, then she leaned in to kiss Jordan on the cheek.

"Hi," she said, almost a whisper. Jordan was still trying to make sense of her presence, let alone the too intimate greeting. No doubt, it had been a bad idea to come here.

"What are you doing here?" She made an effort to sound fairly polite. After all, they had vowed to communicate with each other like adults. Her question was legit. She couldn't imagine Marcus, or anyone else in the department, inviting Bethany.

"For one, my therapist is kicking my ass." Bethany shrugged. "I asked around a bit, took a chance that I might find you here."

"Why do I have the feeling I might not want to be sober for this conversation?"

"Because you're a jaded and suspicious person...and because you're right. Look, Jordan, this isn't easy for me. I didn't come here to win you back though..." She sighed. "I really want to. I understand you need your space. I wanted to apologize."

"Apologize?" Jordan raised a curious eyebrow at her ex-girl-friend. This wasn't something that came easily to Bethany Roberts, FBI profiler and usually the one who thought she had everyone figured out. Bethany had wanted them to do couples' counseling after the abduction. When Jordan dropped out, she continued to see the therapist. They sat down at the bar where Jordan ordered a Long Island Iced Tea, waiting for a comment that didn't come. Bethany chose a Corona.

"Yeah, about that," she said. "Some shrink I am. Doc made me realize something, and it really hurt."

What do you know about hurt? You weren't strung up by your wrists in a sadistic killer's basement. Jordan took a sip of her drink, grateful for having enough presence of mind to keep in the retort. Whenever they tried to tackle difficult subjects, Bethany would make it all about herself, nothing new there. She had to acknowledge though that Bethany was likely to talk about a different kind of hurt.

"I'm sorry about that," Jordan offered.

"Well...I am sorry too. I was so scared of losing you that I lost sight of what I was doing. You never talked a lot about your family, but it was enough I should have bought a clue."

"Dear God." This time, Jordan couldn't hold back the first thought that sprang to mind. "Please, let's not go there—ever. Whatever it is, you're forgiven. Moving on."

"I didn't realize I was borderline abusive to you." Bethany's eyes glistened with tears, and it occurred to Jordan that all the alcohol in the world would not be enough to get her through the confession Bethany thought she needed to make.

"I'm so sorry, Jordan. I didn't mean to repeat a pattern, I was just...I don't even know. I was so mad when you had your affairs, right under my eyes, and I need you to know I didn't mean it. Especially with where we are now."

"It's all right. If that was all..."

From an observer's point of view, it was fascinating how Bethany, on purpose or not, managed to dismantle every process Jordan had made for herself. Okay, she knew that was the alcohol as well as PTSD talking, but it did take a certain level of insensitivity to bring up Jordan's parents in this context. If familial abuse was in the picture, it often bled into adult relationships. Jordan was well aware of the patterns Bethany was talking about, but they didn't apply to her, did they? No. Her birthparents had been neglectful to the point Child Protective Services got involved, but they never laid a hand on her. They had nothing to do with the fact that this doomed relationship had finally blown up in their faces, hers and Bethany's—or had they?

"That's all you have to say?" Bethany asked incredulously.

"What did you expect me to say? I dealt with all of this a long time ago. As you might remember, I have other things on my mind now."

"Okay."

To Jordan's surprise and relief, Bethany relented quickly. "Okay," she echoed. "Thank you. I appreciate this, even though the timing is pretty bad."

"Are you sure you should be working? I heard you're on the Hobbs case. That's a tough one."

Jordan took her time to answer, meanwhile wondering how her glass had gotten empty so fast, or why she felt slightly light-headed. Most of all, she was afraid Bethany had a point. She couldn't screw up her first big case since her abduction.

"They're all tough ones. The shrink—no offense—said it was okay to work. I'm sorry, but frankly, I don't want to discuss any of this with you. I'm going home now. Please, don't call me." Jordan got to her feet before she could change her mind and make decisions she would bitterly regret later, like having another drink, or ending up in Bethany's bed. She might be flattering herself on the latter. Still. She needed to go home, sleep, clear her mind before dealing with Pratt the next day. "Good night."

"Good night," Bethany said in the tone somewhere between hurt and accusatory that was so familiar to Jordan.

She quickly said goodbye to Marcus and Derek and fled before they could ask her any questions, making a detour to the restroom on her way out. At least Bethany didn't follow her. As she washed her hands, the door of a stall opened, and Ellie stepped outside, and for a moment, the world stopped. It wasn't just because their last interaction had left the future wide open. The last time they'd been in here together, they ended up having sex in one of the stalls.

Ellie finally moved and washed her hands in the sink, a blush to her cheeks. That might have been from the memories, or from having a few drinks with her friends earlier.

"You're leaving already?" she asked, a hint of disappointment to her voice.

"Yes. It's been a long day. You guys have fun."

"Sure." There was a hesitation on Ellie's part, as if she intended to say something, or waited for Jordan to change her mind. She wanted to, badly, but here and now was hardly a good place to pick up the pieces. Jordan hoped Ellie would be patient with her a little while longer.

"Okay then," she said. "I'll see you at work." Maybe she was misinterpreting all the signs, and she should let Ellie get on with her life, but Jordan wasn't ready to give up all hope yet.

"Of course." They shared a smile, and then Ellie was gone.

Jordan didn't go home right away, like she knew she should have, and she didn't stop drinking like she knew she should have. She drew the line at encouraging the blonde with the pixie cut two tables away who gave her the eye. Life was complicated enough at the moment, and sex was another complicated subject. Casual encounters had, in the past, seemed like an acceptable short-term solution, but now she felt uncomfortable at the idea.

Jordan hated Jonathan Darby whom she considered responsible, with a passion. She knew whatever happened during those days were only a few bones of the skeleton in her closet. Jordan had been determined not to let him define the rest of her life or choose for her whom she'd share it with. The more time passed, the harder it was to stick to that plan. She was tired, not just from the workday or a multitude of long days since she'd been back to work. It went bone deep. Jordan had no idea how to stop it, but she was certain that her separation from Bethany was a good start—for Bethany's sake and hers. She couldn't even begin to sort out her growing feelings for Ellie, but as long as her life was a mess like this, she'd do her a favor by staying far, far away.

When she left the second bar of the night, the blonde gave her a half shrug as if to say *"Too bad. Your loss."*

You have no idea, Jordan thought. It had to be bad when she continued to have imaginary conversations with people in her head. With a shudder, she remembered a time when that had been her only way of hanging on to her sanity. She managed to keep it together in the cab, until she was home and walked into her bedroom.

Most of the furniture came from the earlier owner who had left her home behind to start a new exciting career in Japan. This was fine with Jordan, since Bethany had bought most for the apartment they had shared together—not because Jordan didn't want to pay for it, but because Bethany had very strict ideas about the kind of surroundings she needed.

Jordan felt so empty she was perfectly okay with a stranger's choices, more so over those of a well-meaning and overbearing relationship partner. Ex-partner. She lay face down on the bed and started to cry, huge shuddering sobs that embarrassed the hell out of her even though no one was there to see it.

She didn't want Bethany back. She needed to be by herself.

The ghosts never asked if their presence was welcome. Even so, Jordan fell asleep at some point, knowing they would follow her into her nightmares.

She woke five minutes before the alarm, toying with the idea of calling in sick, but decided otherwise. A hot shower, a couple of Aspirin and black coffee did patch up her condition enough to be presentable at work. Clothes. Keep it simple. Pratt was the type of guy who'd be leering as soon as a person with a pair of boobs came into his view, and considered any kind of authority, especially held by women, a challenge. She hadn't seen the man in a long time, but it was something she remembered.

Jordan went with black jeans and a grey turtleneck sweater. Then she took a good look at herself and cringed. She was already running too late for the kind of elaborate makeup job she would have needed to cover up the dark circles under her eyes. Did they come from yesterday's binge, or did she not notice before?

Whatever—it was a sunny morning, so sunglasses would not be too suspicious. She just had to make it through the day.

Derek was waiting for her, parked on the curb across from the trailer park where TJ Pratt still lived. If Kathryn and Jim Larson were still around, it wasn't in the hope of finding their daughter. They had never tried after they signed away their parental rights. It was something to be grateful about, Jordan mused.

"I thought you went home early last night," he greeted her, his tone a mix of curiosity and concern. In all the years she'd known him, Derek had never been patronizing. Jordan hoped he wouldn't start.

"TJ Pratt, spent all his life under this address except for when he was convicted for armed robbery and aggravated assault and did time. Shared a cell with Hobbs for about eighteen months, then was released on parole. Hobbs escaped two months later."

"I see you don't want me to comment on your fashionable outfit."

"The sun is hurting my eyes," she said wryly.

"I bet. Okay, let's do this."

Pratt opened the door on the fourth or fifth knock, seeming neither surprised nor fazed to find the police at his doorstep. As she could have easily predicted, he gave Jordan a thorough once over, with just a quick glance at Derek.

"I expected you earlier," he said. "Come on in. I have nothing to hide."

Jordan wrinkled her nose at the smell of cigarettes and booze, her stomach doing a slight flip. She noticed today's newspaper on a stained folding table. Next to it sat a can of beer and an overflowing ashtray. Just a few minutes, she reminded herself. They'd be out of here in no time.

"I suppose you heard about your former cell mate?" Jordan asked, still looking around the confined space. Pratt didn't offer them a seat, but she wouldn't have sat on any surface in here anyway.

"Hobbs made a run for it," he said matter-of-factly. "Sure. I watch the news, you know. Next you're going to ask me if I've seen him."

"Have you?" Derek cut in.

Pratt shrugged. "You can imagine my P.O. wouldn't be too happy about it, and I really want him to be happy. If Hobbs showed up here, I'd tell him to get the fuck away from me. I believe he's on his way to Mexico."

"Did he ever mention that to you while you were cell mates? Mexico, or his escape plans?" She finally made herself meet his gaze.

"Lady, I don't know what you think it's like on the inside, but everyone has those plans. Most of us just sit it out. I guess he wasn't that patient."

"So did he or didn't he?"

Whatever he deducted from her impatient tone, it made him grin. Pratt was a far cry from the charming, intelligent predator Darby, but they had something in common all the same. The realization triggered a flight response. Jordan had enough therapy sessions under her belt to recognize it as such and not give in to the impulse to shrink away and run, but she had already shown too much.

"He might have mentioned Mexico a couple of times. See, this is the reason why you don't listen to stuff like that. The police think you're a witness. Guys like him think you told on them, and they come back to slit your throat. I don't know anything, so you can just as well stop wasting your time, and mine."

"You're busy with what?" Derek asked.

"Didn't you listen? I'm a good guy these days, looking for a job." He picked up the newspaper and opened it. Indeed, there were some ads circled in the job section. Another long look to Jordan. "You better find this guy soon. He's one sick son of a bitch, gets off on pain."

"Really? I thought you didn't listen to him all that much?"

"Just a fair warning, for old times' sake." His grin widened. "You watch yourself around Hobbs. He doesn't like chicks who talk back to him."

"Yeah well, thanks for that. If he tries to contact you, let us know."

She put a card on the table, careful not to touch the surface. Pratt had noticed, amused at her behavior. He picked up the card and regarded it.

"Homicide? That's...something."

"Hobbs already injured two people during his escape, one of them died. We want to make sure he won't have the chance to take more lives." Jordan knew that was not the answer he'd been hoping for. Some things never changed. She wouldn't let him get to her.

"Hey, I get you, this is bad. I never killed anyone."

"Good for you," she said, and to Derek, "Come on, let's go."

Derek waited until they were back in the car before he said, "What the hell was that all about?"

"Pratt used to hang out with my parents," Jordan said with a shrug. She could tell from the baffled look Derek gave her that he didn't quite follow.

"Somehow I have trouble seeing that."

"A different set of parents," she explained, thinking that the end of the day couldn't come soon enough. "My biological ones, to be correct. When I was twelve, Child Protective Services finally realized they weren't too great to be around, so I ended up in the system and got lucky eventually. No, Mom and Dad don't have that kind of friends." She laughed wryly. Derek was right. The thought that the kind-hearted quiet people that became her foster parents could be in any way associated with Pratt, was absurd. Derek had met them in the hospital in the aftermath of a time Jordan was trying hard to forget. She hadn't called them in a while either.

However, Derek was suspiciously silent now, probably going over Pratt's rap sheet in his mind.

"Not today, okay?" she said. "I think I've revealed enough for the past few days."

At first, she thought he wasn't going to answer to that, but he simply took his time to weigh his words.

"You don't have to be on this case. In fact, you shouldn't. Everyone will understand. It's not your fault that the moment you come back, Hobbs escapes and he turns out to have some sort of connection with someone from your past."

Jordan snorted. "He's not from my past. I haven't spoken to my biological parents in over twenty years, and that's just fine with me. I'm fine."

She might not be fine after work, or in the general sense, but Jordan was certain about one thing. She could do her job and bring Hobbs back behind bars. That was all that counted, in her humble opinion.

⁂

Jordan took a deep breath, content with the sensations, the scent of a familiar perfume, warm skin against hers, a strand of hair tickling her cheek. Ellie. She had missed her so much. She'd been fooling herself, thinking she could stay away from her. Her noble reasons didn't stand the test of reality anyway. Ellie was a grown woman, and she knew what she was getting herself into, more than Jordan wished she would. The same man who had abducted Jordan had attacked her one night on her way home, with one difference—Ellie had gotten away. Sooner, anyway.

There was an abrupt change, turning the sweet flowery scent to something coppery, her hand touching liquid. When her eyes snapped open, instead of Ellie, she saw him, grinning at her as he shook his head.

"My, Jordan, did you really think it would be this easy?"

Jordan jolted awake, spending a few minutes on the verge of hyperventilating before the paralyzing effect of the nightmare vanished and she could breathe properly again. Certain she wouldn't get any more sleep, she got up and walked into her kitchen where she switched on the light above the stove. She didn't mind the silence or relative darkness that came with living outside of the city.

Darkness and silence didn't scare her. The monsters were lurking in her mind.

You must know you were my favorite. He'd try to get to her even after his arrest, and obviously, it still worked perfectly. Jordan sighed and turned on the faucet, pouring herself a glass of ice-cold water. The smell and taste of blood lingered.

She wasn't fine.

There was no way in hell she'd call Bethany and rip even more old wounds open. Jordan didn't mind the games Bethany had played to try and lure Darby out of hiding. Brilliant minds often walked a fine line, and what she had done was risky, but not even completely outside the book. This was something Jordan understood. To get a women-hating creep off the streets, the purpose justified almost every means. It had been bad luck for Jordan that she got caught in the crossfire, and Darby had fooled her too.

Her fingers clenched around the edge of the sink as she struggled to remain in the present, not to give in to the real sensations of nausea that came with the memory. Going back to the trailer park and talking to Pratt had shaken her like she knew it would. She couldn't afford to let it show too much. Her job, even considering the triggers that came with it, kept her sane. She needed sane, because otherwise, she might do something ill-considered, irreversible one day.

Jordan considered going in right this moment, until she remembered that this was the first of her two days off. She had craved time to herself, but all of a sudden, the prospect looked terrifying.

Once upon a time, she'd had a mostly functioning set of coping strategies, not all of them terribly functional, but they worked. At least, they had worked so far, but both intimacy and a few relaxing dreams came with the potential loss of control…She hadn't lived with a psychiatrist for nothing. She knew her patterns. At this point, all Jordan wanted was for the noise to stop, and that was something she hadn't achieved even in the stillness of her home.

She didn't know how.

Chapter Two

"So, what's new with you?" Jensen Baker asked when they drove back to the station.

Ellie wasn't sure whether she appreciated her partner's attempt at small talk. She was tired after a double shift, and there wasn't much she could tell him anyway. Jensen, however, had great news. He and his girlfriend Kate were getting married. Jensen, Kate, and Ellie had all graduated from the academy the same year, and they got to work together every now and then. She wondered what had happened—it seemed like she'd blinked, and all of her friends were getting married. Libby Marshall had dated a detective for some time now, Kate and Jensen were together. Ellie had thrown herself head over heels into an affair with gorgeous, but troubled—not to mention, taken—Jordan Carpenter. While it was none of Jensen's business, the whole department already knew more than she ever cared to reveal to her colleagues. Gossip traveled fast, and Dr. Bethany Roberts, the scorned woman in this scenario, wasn't known for keeping a low profile.

Ellie hoped to take the detective's exam the next year, but that wasn't news either. She still needed a roommate to pay for the higher rent since her ex had moved out months ago, but as someone newly engaged, he sure couldn't help with that.

"Nothing, really." There had been a moment when Ellie had seriously considered asking Jordan if she wanted to move in with her, become roommates, with or without benefits, her choice. That was before she learned Jordan had bought a house, something she had kept from both her longtime girlfriend and her lover (though Ellie might overestimate herself using that term). It wasn't easy to understand Jordan Carpenter. It had been too damn easy to fall for her.

Presently, Ellie had to decide whether she should hang on or move on—which was hard to do when they weren't talking, and she knew Jordan was still working through the recent trauma of having been abducted by a serial killer.

Ellie shuddered. She'd seen the basement. It didn't take much to put together the clues. After her own attack, Ellie had craved and sought a human connection, something to make her feel alive. As for Jordan, it seemed like she needed distance and solitude instead. No, there was nothing new.

"That's not necessarily a bad thing," Jensen commented, and Ellie had to agree. She was grateful he didn't try to break the surface of small talk too much. It was different between women. Kate might have asked questions Ellie wasn't able to answer.

"Yeah." She didn't know what else to say. Lucky for her—not so much the person involved—the message from dispatch interrupted their stalling conversation. A likely disoriented woman had been spotted walking on the highway, endangering herself and drivers. There had already been a couple of minor accidents. They were close. Ellie answered the call, and they were on their way.

Two ambulances and another squad car had arrived before them. Paramedics were already attending to a woman in her twenties who had been aimlessly staggering into traffic. Together with the other officers, they managed to block off a stretch of the highway and close one lane. Ellie approached the woman, who was dressed for a casual office workday, carefully.

"Miss? Let's get you off the street. It's too dangerous."

The terror in the woman's gaze was unmistakable, but she let Ellie lead her away and to the ambulance. Holding her arm, Ellie could feel her shaking hard.

"He took my car," she said, tears streaming down her face.

Ellie took in the red ligature marks around her wrists and the bruise on the side of her face, and thought the car was probably not the worst loss the woman had suffered today. You went through your life most days unaware of the bad things that could happen—until they happened to you, or someone you cared about.

"Can you tell me your name, and what happened?" she asked, keeping her voice soft and reassuring. The anger washing through her wouldn't help the woman, or anyone, for that matter, although she couldn't deny it was there, or where it came from.

"Marley Gordon," the woman said, her voice still barely above a whisper. "I was at the organic supermarket, in the parking lot. He pulled a gun on me and forced me to drive. I was so scared!"

"I can imagine," Ellie said, not simply to reassure Marley Gordon, but because she could. "You're safe now. I'm going to need the license plate of your car so we can find him."

"Okay. He...he took my purse, with everything in it. Please find him."

"I'll take care of this," Jensen promised after Marley had recited the numbers and letters. "You go to the hospital with her?"

Ellie nodded.

"I need to call my husband...oh my God...who's going to get the children from daycare?" Overwhelmed with questions, Marley started to cry.

"Don't worry, Ms. Gordon. We'll go to the hospital now, and we'll notify your husband as well." Ellie climbed into the back of the ambulance with the paramedic, a tall blonde woman. She continued, "Could you describe the man some more, anything you remember, hair color, clothes, anything specific?"

"I was so scared," Marley repeated, clearly close to the end of her line. The paramedic's expression was stormy, but she didn't comment on Ellie's line of questioning, aware that it was necessary.

"I know." Ellie tried not to think of the moment she had woken in the hospital, her own colleagues eager to question her about the man who had attacked her on her way home.

"He had...brown hair, I guess. He was wearing jeans and a plaid shirt. Fifties maybe. He looked...rugged."

"Did he ever tell you his name, or where he wanted to go?"

"No, but his face looked familiar somehow. I don't know. Maybe I saw him on TV somewhere. Is that possible?"

Ellie had formed a suspicion. Could it be too much of a coincidence? The description Gordon gave was vague, but it fit the man whose spectacular prison escape had made headlines almost a week ago. Phil Hobbs. Jordan and her partner Derek Henderson had joined roll call to inform the uniformed officers about the situation, but the felon hadn't resurfaced since then. If he had taken Gordon's car, it meant he was still in the area.

"I believe so," she said, troubled. Hobbs had injured two people during his escape, one guard still in critical condition the other one dead. All things considered, Gordon was lucky. "Excuse me. I have to make a call."

When she detailed her suspicion to Sergeant Bristol, he told her to go to the hospital with Gordon.

Ellie had expected that a detective on Hobbs' case would meet her there. Since this was an all hands on deck effort, she was still surprised and a bit nervous when she realized who waited for her outside the ER. *Stay professional.*

"He tied her up in the car, and when she asked him not to kill her, he hit her. Eventually though, he let her out on the side of the road. When she told me he looked familiar, I thought this might not be a coincidence."

"Good call," Jordan said. In spite of the dire situation, Ellie felt warmed by her praise. She was still somewhat startled to see Jordan here, though she shouldn't have been. It was Jordan's first case after the abduction. Of course she'd have Derek call her if there was any development, even on her off day.

Not that Ellie heard a lot from Jordan herself lately. She listened carefully to anything colleagues said in the department, in and in between the lines. She felt a bit like a stalker that way, but she wasn't willing to let go yet.

"Thanks," she said. "Let's hope this will be over soon."

"Yeah." Jordan seemed to want to add something to that, and Ellie held her breath, as if anything other than catching a violent felon could count right now. Then her cell phone rang, and she excused herself.

Ellie watched her from a few feet away, mixed emotions tearing her into every which direction. She, like Jordan, saw the job as #1 priority. Neither of them would cave because of roadblocks along the way—but there was something else between them harder to define. The question whether they still had a chance, or ever had one to begin with, was weighing on her mind. Ellie wanted no detours in the career she had planned for a long time. She wanted Jordan. It was uncertain whether she could have it all.

"Hobbs was caught on the surveillance camera of a gas station," Jordan, who had finished the call, told her. "Let's go."

"Wait...Shouldn't I go back to the station, report to—"

"You report to me for now," Jordan said curtly. "It's cleared with Sergeant Bristol."

"Oh. Okay then."

Jordan studied her for a moment, and sighed, before she said, "Let's keep it about the job, okay? I know we should talk, and we will, soon. Now's not the time."

"Sure. I understand."

Ellie meant it. Jordan was right. Their private story was of little relevance at the moment. That didn't mean she wasn't disappointed, and at the same time thrilled that Jordan seemed to want to keep that door open. At Marcus's retirement party, she and Bethany hadn't left together.

It was better than nothing.

❧

Hobbs had abandoned Marley Gordon's car on the side of the road. Whether or not he had continued on foot was unclear. They found it about a mile from the gas station which was curious—Hobbs was a hardened, experienced criminal. He wouldn't realize only a mile later that he'd been caught on tape and leave a car with the tank he just filled, that could have brought him much further. It was almost like he wanted to let the police know he was around, though that didn't make any sense.

Then again, he'd been on the run for a few days now with probably very few resources. The mess in Marley Gordon's Honda was an indication he had gone through her groceries. Ellie watched Jordan wrinkle her nose as she leaned into the driver's seat.

"Cigarettes and booze?" she said. "He didn't get that from the gas station, according to the clerk."

Ellie frowned. "Gordon was shopping at an organic store...she didn't seem the type to smoke and drink the hard stuff. So, he stopped somewhere else?"

"Not a lot of time lapsed between the gas station and when he dumped the car, and no further hits on Gordon's credit card." Jordan leaned in again, taking out a crumpled can of beer with a gloved hand. "Damn."

"I know what you're thinking. Pratt's favorite brand." Derek Henderson had joined them, and obviously he remembered the packs of cigarettes they'd seen at Pratt's as well. "You could be right. We might have to pay him another visit."

Ellie could sense that might wasn't good enough for Jordan.

"Especially if we find his prints on here. He's hiding in plain sight! What if Mexico was a red herring Pratt fed us?"

The senior detective's gaze was doubtful, and even Ellie had to admit it was a long shot.

"Come on guys, don't rain on my parade." To another uniformed officer, Jordan said, "I want all prints you get off this. Check for Thomas Jeffrey Pratt. Start with the cans and cigarette pack. That's priority! Any connection you can find, you call me right away."

"Yes, Ma'am."

"Where can he go from here?" Henderson's question was partly rhetorical. A person could easily get lost in the stretch of woods in front of them, but how far could they make it without shelter or support?

"I guess we have to find out," Jordan said. "Let's get a search team together. I'll keep my favorite rookie. I want someone to keep an eye on the trailer park. It's your turn to ask the lieutenant."

Derek gave half an eye roll. "How long until you'll forgive me for the baby puke? Not my fault they sent you." He got on the phone without further protest though. Roadblocks would be put in place, the woods combed thoroughly. Hobbs had been lucky so far, but his luck was about to run out.

Ellie was very much looking forward to that moment. It would look good on her résumé—and Jordan's, something they both could use.

"Baby puke?"

"Don't ask," Jordan warned her.

My favorite rookie. For all her praise, Jordan didn't talk to her much once the search parties were assembled and each team went on their way. Ellie found her enthusiasm vanishing by the minute. They didn't know Hobbs was hiding in here. He could have hitched a ride, had someone else help him or simply vanished off the face of the earth, she thought with frustration.

Marley Gordon had been lucky, but the next person might not be. Her feet hurt in the newly issued shoes she'd been wearing for about a week now, not that it was something important in the grand scheme of things. It was the kind of pain easy to forget, unlike others. They worked in silence, everyone hoping for the crucial clue. The sky was beginning to cloud over, and soon the first drops fell, turning into a downpour within moments. The frustration among the investigators was palpable—if there were any traces to be found, they'd vanish soon in the pouring rain. Minutes turned into hours. Soon, daylight would fade into night.

The only call Jordan got during that time made her sigh and hang up on the caller with an unhappy expression.

"Apparently, Hobbs' prints were on the pack and the cans, but not Pratt's. That's not possible."

"Why do you think Pratt helped him?" Ellie asked and preventively held up her hands. "I know, they were cell mates for a while, but Pratt was already out. What reason could he have to risk associating himself with the guy?"

"Intimidation, money. We're looking into that." Jordan's tone said clearly how useless these lines of investigation had been so far. She was tense, getting more so by the minute. They were coming up empty once more. "He's a freaking chameleon. I can't believe we came so close and didn't get him."

"He'll show up again."

"Let's hope. Are you okay?"

Ellie really wasn't, but she would survive. They both had survived worse. She wouldn't complain about a tight shoe in front of a woman who had gotten away from a serial killer. At least, she was determined not to.

"I'm fine. Let's get this done before it gets dark."

They had help from a team in a helicopter flying over the vast area, but Hobbs remained hidden.

Marley Gordon being alive still made it a good day in everyone's book, but that didn't help with the frustration of the investigators.

Jordan was still in the lieutenant's office with Henderson when Ellie's shift ended. She declined joining a group of co-workers for a drink and sat in a café across from the department instead, nursing a black coffee in the hope that the conversation Jordan had hinted at could take place tonight. No such luck. After a little over an hour, Ellie went home. They were working together again. She'd have to settle for that.

Chapter Three

Her first stop after work was the 24/7 gym. As soon as her recovery allowed, Jordan had made it a daily habit. She was working tirelessly on getting herself back into the mindset prior to her captivity and making sure her body got the memo too. The doctor had assured her that Darby's knack for medieval torture methods hadn't left any permanent damage. Any remaining pain had to be solely psychological.

Then, there were the recurring nightmares slowing down her desired progress. You'd think it had to be cold in a basement like that, instead the air had been stuffy, the fabric of what little clothes she'd had on her sticking to her clammy skin. An intense work-out was an almost foolproof strategy to fall into a near comatose sleep later, and, even more important to assure herself that she wasn't weak, yielding, like Darby had hoped. Pushing her limits kept him at bay, something Jordan was grateful for.

When she returned home, there were two calls, one from Bethany she deleted without listening—self-care—and one from Pauline and Jack who asked her to come to dinner on the weekend after next.

Jordan sat on the couch, for a moment forgetting about the pressure of finding Hobbs, or the unholy connection with TJ Pratt. Fortunately, the couple whom she considered her real parents, had never learned too many details of what happened in Darby's basement, but they worried. She had done her best to keep them at bay too. That was actually something Bethany had helped with—they didn't know about the breakup yet. Jordan knew Pauline and Jack had been uncomfortable when she was around. Jordan, not exactly good at keeping people who cared about her, close, hadn't intervened.

So yes, she owed them dinner at least. Maybe Ellie would come. She needed someone to fence off the questions, and while Bethany would certainly volunteer, she was also the last person on earth Jordan wanted to ask. That could work.

After another few indecisive moments, she got to her feet, put her coat back on and went outside. The wind had turned, and Jordan shivered in the colder air. She was certain Pratt hadn't told her everything, and never would with any of her colleagues around. Whether or not he could lead them to Hobbs was unclear, but there was something unfinished.

Old habits died hard...Pratt still lived in the same trailer park, so it wasn't much of a stretch to assume he would still visit the same shady places. Not all of the bars in walking distance to the park were still around, but a few had been in the area forever. A single woman would get odd, leering looks in all of them, no surprise there. Jordan hit pay dirt on the second one, a run-down bar called "Jerry's".

She wondered if there were still people playing cards in the back room. Her birthparents had been buddies with the owner, now it was Jerry junior running the place. It was still cheap and dirty. Jordan wished she could claim overtime pay for going after a hunch. However, she needed to stay under the radar for the time being, not make too many waves and have anyone make this about her and her ability to do the job rather than the re-capture of a dangerous criminal.

Pratt sat at the bar. Trying not to let the disgust show in her expression, for him, for this place, she sat next to him and ordered a beer.

"This is police harassment," he complained.

"Right. Cheers, TJ. You hang out with my dad lately?"

His laughter made her skin crawl. "Why do you want to know? You thought you were too good for your folks, huh? What makes you think they want anything to do with you now?"

She shrugged and turned her attention to her beer. "Just making small talk, you know. Maybe you and Phil did too. Eight months is a long time. Maybe something's finally jogging your memory."

"I told you, I have no idea where he is. You must be desperate."

It was a good thing he didn't know how much.

"We don't know yet how you helped him change cars, but we will find out. Your P.O.'s not going to be happy."

He scoffed. "You are crazy. Are you even listening to me? I haven't talked to him. I want nothing to do with Hobbs. Wow, that guy really did a number on you, didn't he?"

"What the hell are you talking about?"

A smug smile spread on his face. "I read the newspaper, remember? Didn't see that one coming, he looked so normal."

Jordan wasn't going to discuss one criminal with another.

"I don't like you, but I swear if you help us get to him, we will work something out. For old times sake, if you will."

That seemed to amuse him. "You know what they say about trailer trash, don't you? I don't trust you, Jordan. Get lost. I'm sure you're enjoying your new life, and don't want your colleagues to find out too much about the old one. You want stories, I've got some to tell."

"I hope you're not trying to threaten me, because that wouldn't be a smart move. You want a pissing contest, TJ? Remember, I'm a detective now and you...are just the guy who might have helped an escaped convict. It looks much better for one of us."

She tossed a bill on the counter and stood. "Have a good night."

He swore under his breath. Jordan didn't need to be a mind-reader to tell there was a gendered slur involved.

What she'd done was risky, and pretty much outside the book, but Jordan hadn't felt this good in forever. She was still confident that if they continued to lean harder on Pratt, they might shake something loose. So far, Hobbs' flight seemed successful, if chaotic. They had to concentrate on the chaotic part. He would make a mistake. He couldn't hide out in the woods forever, and there were no other known associates—the people he had committed crimes with were either in prison or dead, that was the kind of company he kept. They would get him.

Much consoled by those thoughts, Jordan went back home and to bed, having the first good night's sleep in a long time cut short by Derek's call.

"Really? This was supposed to be the second of my two days off. What happened to that?" She wasn't serious. If Derek called her at this time, that could only mean there was news. The idea excited her. "All right, good or bad?"

"Good, I hope," he said. "Pratt is here. He says he wants talk to you."

"What? Why?"

"He looked pretty beat up, doesn't want to go to a hospital though. He says he went out for a couple of drinks, and when he came back to the trailer, Hobbs was waiting for him and jumped him. Somebody heard the commotion, and Hobbs fled. We have officers at the scene right now."

That still didn't explain why Pratt wanted to talk to her. Jordan had the unsettling thought that he held back their earlier encounter for a reason. It wasn't something he could use against her—she'd followed a hunch on her off time, and she was free to go wherever she wanted, even if that meant a rundown bar like Jerry's.

"I'll be there in..." Ten, she'd almost said, but of course that wasn't possible. She still hadn't gotten used to counting in the longer commute. "Just wait for me."

"Jordan, before we get started here...is there anything else I need to know?"

"No, why?" Her denial was swift and hopefully credible.

"He seems to take an interest in you. Him, knowing your parents, could that be in any way connected? Should we talk to them?"

"He's a jerk, that's all. Look, I need to get ready. I'll see you."

Jordan ended the conversation by punching the end call button. This was going to be uncomfortable, no doubt about it. Her comfort didn't matter at the moment—if Pratt could help them to determine Hobbs' whereabouts, it was worth a small sacrifice.

She showered and dressed quickly, then, with her hair still damp, picked up her keys and jacket. A floorboard creaked underneath her shoes when she passed by the dining area. The former owner had nice furniture, even though some parts of the house and décor were a bit dated. She might do a little do-over soon, make it more her own. There was some sort of a future for her, and it might include a pretty blonde rookie who had risked her career and life to save Jordan's. She had to remember that.

⁕

Jordan knew the moment she walked into the interrogation room that something wasn't right. Pratt looked exactly like Derek had described, a bruise on his neck that could very well stem from someone attacking him from behind, a bandage around his arm.

"Good morning, Detective," he said, giving her a wink. Pratt's smile, his posture, all of it was too cocky, too confident. He didn't look like a man who was scared, either of going back to prison, or a vengeful Hobbs coming after him.

"Took you some time to get here. That doesn't look like you're eager to solve the case. Seems to me like you're distracted, but I'm sure everyone understands after what you've been through. Do you still have nightmares? Poor thing."

"Cut the bullshit," Jordan shot back at him, then took a deep breath. She sat down across from him. "What's all this about?" she asked.

"Hey, you came to me. Not once, but twice—but I guess your colleagues already told you why I'm here. Hobbs came by, and, as you can see, not for a friendly talk."

She winced at his reference to the previous night. Of course, she couldn't have hoped to keep it a secret—then so be it. Finding Hobbs was more important, though something about this story felt off to her.

"I came to you in the hope that your memory would improve over time. So, you fed us a load of shit, like you did when you told us Hobbs was on his way to Mexico?"

"That's what he said at the time, hey, I'd prefer if he'd stuck to it. The son of a bitch wanted to kill me." Pratt shrugged. "It doesn't matter anymore. I want protection before I tell you anything else."

"Protection? For what?"

"You're serious? I went out for a couple of drinks last night *as you know*, and when I came back, he had broken into my house.

The place was a mess, and I knew what that meant. Before I could get out, he jumped me. If it wasn't for that kid, I would be dead!"

Jordan sent a questioning look towards the two-way mirror. A witness? She still wasn't convinced that Pratt was the innocent victim in this story.

"Two days ago, you went out of your way trying to convince us that there's no connection between him and you. Why would he come back here when you two hardly ever talked? If you have nothing to share with the police, why would he take the risk?"

"Are you stupid?" For the first time, his composure was slipping. "That guy is nuts! This means something, and I can assure you, it's not good. Him doing this, a couple of days after you guys showed up, I don't think that's a coincidence."

"Why are you so sure it's Hobbs and not one of your neighbors?" Jordan knew she was risking being called stupid again, but based on her own memories, it wouldn't be such a surprise in the neighborhood. She thought it was likely that Hobbs was sending a message to his former cell mate, but she wanted to be sure.

"You know this crowd. I assume you know the difference between a simple break-in and one that has a deeper meaning, sending a message—or else you're just a lousy detective. I might just remember more of what he said when we were in the joint if you make sure he's not going to kill me."

Jordan shook her head. "Nope, doesn't work that way." She got to her feet.

"Hey, wait, where are you going? I thought you want this guy!"

"I'll be back in two minutes," she said. "Then you're going to tell me everything you know, and we can talk about what we can do for you. You try to play games with me now, there'll be no deal. In fact, I'm still not sure whether he just didn't come back to touch base with an old buddy who could help him hide."

"You are crazy!" he exclaimed.

Jordan smiled at him. "Hey. *You* came to me." Then she left the room.

Outside, Henderson stood with his arms crossed over his chest. He didn't need anything else to convey his disapproval to Jordan. She sighed.

"I know, not my best, but I swear we're getting there. You believe him?"

"He looks pretty beaten up, that's for sure." Derek's answer was slightly evasive. "Fact is if Hobbs came back, he has a reason."

"What about that witness he's talking about?"

"Dean Johnson, a kid who lives in the park."

"Okay, let's go talk to him. If a crime occurred like Pratt says, and I'm still not convinced of that...maybe we'll find something else, related to Hobbs or not."

"Related to Hobbs or not," he repeated. "What is it about this guy? He's rattling you."

"I'll tell my therapist all about it," she joked. "Now let's get some work done."

"Jordan," he tried again.

"Did you hear what I just said? Someone needs to take a look at that trailer, and I have to get back in there for a moment."

"I mean it. If you want to talk..."

The terrible magic word, and the last she wanted to hear from him right now. How hard was it to not treat her like something fragile, like she was going to break any moment? He meant well. Everyone did, even Bethany. It was driving her crazy.

"There's no time right now. Maybe we can get a drink after work." Without a further word, she went back into the room, where Pratt's stance was a little less cocky now.

"So?"

He groaned. "I don't trust you, but I guess I have no choice. Hobbs didn't talk much in prison, but we ran into each other before. On the outside. Same old group, with your parents and some friends. See, most of us wanted to do a little dope and leave it at that, but he was always going on about something bigger."

Of all the stories, Jordan hadn't expected that. A possible connection to her birthparents made this case go downhill very fast, the mere thought giving her a headache. As far as she knew, they'd had a few run-ins with the police, before and after she'd left, but nothing major. They weren't the type of people she dealt with in her day job.

Then again, she was still trying to convince herself that neglect wasn't abuse. Maybe she'd been wrong. Maybe she was wrong again.

"I didn't think he was serious at the time," Pratt continued. "Someone who gets out needs to get away as soon as he can...He once mentioned getting back at those who didn't support his plans. I remember your dad told him flat out he was crazy, and he didn't like to hear that. He might come after someone, and I don't want to take that risk."

There it was, that sleazy smile again, telling Jordan that Pratt had other things on this mind than his concern for Hobbs' plans. "It might do some good and help reunite a family. You know your mom was really upset after Child Protective Services took you away."

"That's heartbreaking." If her birthparents had been upset, it certainly wasn't because of that, but the drugs the police had confiscated at the scene. "All right. We'll take a look around, see if there's anything to help us find Hobbs. You'll get your wish."

"Well, thank you. I knew you would come around...for old times' sake if nothing else."

"It's not like you gave us something big. However, it's a start. I wouldn't want Hobbs to come around and take care of all the loose ends he thinks are still out there."

Pratt shook his head. "Are you even listening? You and your family are some of those loose ends."

"If you say so. Well, thanks for the talk," Jordan said and got to her feet, grateful she didn't have to share space and air with him any longer. "I'll have someone contact your P.O., and we'll go from here."

Derek was waiting for her outside. He was clearly still mulling over something. Jordan didn't like that it was most likely her family connections. If it came to that, she might still want off the case. This had nothing to do with Darby, but it was a memory lane she didn't want to go down.

"All right, let's go check this out."

"Marshall and Baker are over there right now, as well as the crime scene unit," he said. "Let's hope they'll find something."

"Yeah."

"Is it time to contact your parents?" Derek asked. "From what he said, they might be in danger too, and you could be as well."

Jordan shook her head. "He might believe that, but I don't. Hobbs is too smart to get caught in old revenge schemes, and for what? Look, Pratt is right, all they wanted to do is get high. Hobbs is not going to lose precious time over some potheads, and risk going back to prison. This thing with Pratt, it seems more personal."

"Let's not take the risk. You want to take him to a safe house?"

"Sure. Let him stew a little, make him see we have better offers than Hobbs," she said, somewhat irritated he didn't share her assessment.

Derek cast a long look at Pratt on the other side of the glass, then he nodded. "All right. Let's go over to the trailer park and see if the kids have anything for us."

On their way out, Jordan stopped in her tracks at the sight of Ellie at the front desk, hesitating, unsure.

"You're coming?"

"Can you give me a minute?"

"No problem." Derek walked a few steps further waited in a respectful distance next to the entrance.

"Hi, Ellie," Jordan said.

Ellie who had her gaze fixed to the computer screen jumped a little. "Jordan. Hi. Can I help you with anything?"

Given the past rather crappy few days, with the exemption of one dream that had quickly turned into a bloody nightmare, Jordan was happy to take in the sight of her, the slightly messy ponytail and the soft blush—in the silence between them, memories came easily. Maybe it was the same for Ellie, because her blush deepened, and she looked down at a sheet on her keyboard. Jordan remembered that she had asked her a question.

"Will you be at the *Code 7* tonight?"

Ellie cast a quick, surprised glance her way. Jordan couldn't blame her for that. She had kept her distance best she could, despite her promise that they'd talk. Apparently, she wasn't as good at it as she'd thought. She was lonely—but before she could involve Ellie in any of this, she owed her the truth, make sure she knew what she was getting herself into. After that, Ellie could decide whether she was still interested in pursuing a relationship.

"I don't know, maybe. You?"

"Unless something comes up, yes. I'd like to ask you something."

Across the hall, Derek pointed at his watch. "Later. We need to head over to Pratt's again. He claims Hobbs broke into his trailer, tried to kill him. If that's the truth, hopefully he left some traces."

"Okay. Good luck. I'll see you later," Ellie said with a hopeful smile.

"Looking forward to it. Bye."

Joining her partner again, Jordan had almost forgotten about what Pratt said to her, but it came back to her quickly enough. On the bright side, she hadn't obsessed about Darby and how she should have seen through him sooner, for a few hours.

Small favors. She appreciated them.

❦

"This is Dean Johnson," Officer Marshall introduced the lanky teenager to Jordan and Derek. "Detectives Carpenter and Henderson. Could you tell them what you saw?"

The young man was fidgeting, his hands in his back pockets. "Man, that was crazy. I was just walking past, and all of a sudden, I heard them fighting, things breaking...then the guy came out, and he was running."

"You got a good look at him?" Jordan asked. Marshall looked a tad skeptical, she realized.

"Absolutely. It was the guy they showed on the news, who escaped from prison. I saw his face."

"Why didn't you call the police?"

"TJ said I didn't have to because he was going to, and that I should just wait. Did I do anything wrong?"

"No, that's fine." Jordan turned away from his wide-eyed expression, impatient, with him, with herself, because she couldn't figure out if he was lying. Why would he? It wasn't like Pratt had any riches to promise. "You can go to the station with Officer Marshall, and she'll take your statement."

"That'll be it?"

"That'll be it," she confirmed, "unless you remember something else. TJ said it was last night when the fight happened…It's dark around here, right?"

"There was a light on in the trailer, and when the door opened, I had a clear look of his face. I swear to you, it was Hobbs."

"Did he see you?"

"I don't think so. I hid when I realized who he was. Then I went to check on TJ. Hobbs tried to strangle him, and he was bleeding from a cut in his arm."

"You saw the knife?"

"No. I assume Hobbs brought it with him and took it when he left."

"That's what TJ told you?" Derek asked.

"Yes, but why would he make that up? He was freaking out, and man, I would too if someone tried to kill me."

"Fair enough. Thank you, Dean. Officer Marshall will take it from here."

"It's odd," Jordan said after they'd both stepped into the trailer.

"What is?"

"All of it." She took in the mess, turned over furniture, broken glass. "Why would he come back here?"

"You heard Pratt," Derek said as he was taking a closer look at a bloodstain on the carpet.

"He tried to strangle him first, then stab him? I don't know. That sounds awfully unorganized."

"He doesn't have a lot of time or means to be organized," Derek reminded her. "Maybe Pratt is exaggerating, and Hobbs just wanted to send him a warning not to talk to the police—which he did. What was that about last night anyway?"

Jordan shrugged, turned away from her partner. She didn't care to discuss this subject in depth. "I had a hunch. Last night, he wasn't as willing to talk though. Maybe you're right and he's really scared now. I just don't see it."

"What else would be his motivation? If he wanted Hobbs to get away, he didn't need to come in. I think this could help to draw Hobbs out."

"Hm."

"Hm, what?"

"I hope you're right," Jordan said. She still wasn't sure whether to believe Pratt, even with the obvious commotion that had taken place here. Her hesitation could be from experience, or paranoia. It was hard to tell.

Chapter Four

Earlier that morning, Ellie had been disappointed to be assigned to the front desk, but she didn't mind it so much now that there was a ray of sun after weeks of constant grey. It was hard to uphold her enthusiasm when it felt like she was the only one. Jordan wanted to meet, for drinks, and talk. This was big. It was the moment she'd been waiting for.

In fact, she was now glad to sit behind a computer instead of the wheel of a squad car.

Everything had been chaotic for a while after Jordan's ordeal, and Ellie's own nightmares didn't help. Bethany Roberts had made an attempt to get back together, work things out, but Jordan opted out of couples' therapy, despite her claim that she owed Bethany. Maybe that meant she was ready to acknowledge she'd paid her dues to her ex—or it could mean something different altogether. Ellie would find out tonight.

The rest of the afternoon passed rather quietly, with no new sighting of Hobbs. Ellie knew Libby and Jensen had been sent to the trailer. She sighed. Yes, at the moment she was preoccupied with what might or might not be a date, something hopeful, but she needed the experience. Of the four of them, Kate, Jensen, and Libby, she had always been the one who knew she wanted to be a detective from day one. She was going to take the exam the moment she'd be eligible.

She needed to keep that goal in mind too, and deal with her housing situation at some point. One step at a time—once it was clear where she and Jordan would go from here, she'd figure out the rest as well.

Another hour, and she was back in civilian gear, ready for whatever the night might bring. The green dress might be a little too much for the bar the co-workers of this precinct usually flocked to, so were the high-heeled sandals. It didn't matter. She knew Jordan appreciated this style on her, and Ellie was done worrying about whether any misogynist asshole would look at her differently for it. She was glad she could listen to the sound of her heels on the pavement without it triggering a flashback.

Worrying about the life of someone you loved had a way of pushing fears for yourself aside. Ellie liked the sound of that: Love. It made her all warm and tingly inside. Jordan was right. They had a lot to talk about—and a lot of guilt to work around. Roberts might have been there for Jordan in a devastating moment, but it wasn't something she could hold over her for the rest of her life.

"Hey, look at you. Hot date tonight?" Kate joked. She'd been in booking today, so they'd only talked on the phone.

"I'm not sure. I'm trying not to make too much of it."

"I see. Detective Carpenter?"

"Not what you think. We'll just hang out, have a couple of drinks if she makes it, which isn't clear yet. Don't you want to come tonight?" It occurred to Ellie that spending the evening with Kate would be a good plan B in case Jordan didn't show up. She hoped that wouldn't happen, but she wasn't certain either.

"Sure, why not? Jensen's still tied up as well, but maybe he and Libby can join us later."

"Great. Let's go. You have to tell me all about how the wedding plans are going, because I suspect Jensen isn't so clear on the details. He didn't say much."

Kate laughed. "Men. All this talk about fonts for the invitations and the exact tone for flowers and decorations and wedding cake...not their strongest suit."

"I imagine. Well, I want to hear all about it. I can't promise I won't be jealous though."

"It's legal for you to marry too, remember?"

"Yeah. I'd have to find someone to marry first," Ellie reminded her. "Now I feel like a drink."

Kate laughed. "Who knows, maybe that person is closer than you think."

Ellie shook her head, amused. That would be a little too much luck to hope for.

Two hours and a couple of drinks later, Ellie snuck a quick glance at her watch, disappointed, but unwilling to lose hope yet. No message. Jordan had said she might be late. Jensen and Libby hadn't yet arrived either.

"Do you *want* to get married someday?" Kate asked. They had been drinking approximately at the same speed, about to cross into the territory of uncomfortable truths. "I'm telling you, the prospect is awesome, and it's terrifying me as well. I mean, Jensen's a great guy. I love him, but what if we disagree on everything, as much as we already do on white versus cream-colored paper for invitations, and butter cream versus chocolate?"

Ellie had drifted a little, so it took her a moment to realize Kate was still talking about cakes. She honestly attempted to think about this dilemma, coming up empty. Since Jordan walked in that moment, she had to give a quick answer.

"You'll figure it out," she said. "It's just nerves. You two will get over it and focus on the big picture."

How could anyone ever know for sure? She wanted to be with Jordan. She had never stopped wanting that, but the future still looked uncertain. Ellie guessed she'd be the wiser soon.

Libby and Jensen came in right after Jordan, and Kate got to her feet. "Hi, Jordan," she greeted the detective. "I better go see what my fiancé is up to."

"Oh, no, you can all stay here," Jordan said. "Ellie and I will be over there."

Just like that, it was decided, but Ellie didn't mind. After all, what Jordan wanted to say to her seemed to require some privacy. She was all right with that.

They sat down, partially hidden behind a column—almost romantic. The chatter and laughter of their colleagues faded into the background.

"Don't you want to get a drink?" Ellie asked. She noticed that her voice sounded like a breathless rasp, and she didn't mind. She had waited so long for this second chance. It was almost like starting from scratch, the complicated but incredibly pleasant moments they had spent together like a distant dream.

"In a moment. Look, Ellie...," Jordan began. "I'm aware I've been avoiding you these past weeks, and busy or not, it wasn't fair to you."

"It's okay. You needed that time." Ellie barely kept herself from fidgeting, and she was aware of her rapid heartbeat.

"Yeah. I guess. This case, with Hobbs, it's stirring up some bad stuff. I have a lot on my plate right now."

"I know." Despite her excitement that this conversation was finally happening, Ellie stayed guarded, keeping her defenses up. At this point, she might still walk out of here with a broken heart, or not spend the night alone after all. "That's okay, I understand. I don't mean to rush you. I never...I'd just like to know where we stand," she finished, unsure whether she made it clear how much she wanted them to be together again, better, have a new start. Jordan had some heavy issues to deal with, but so did Ellie. She knew what it was like—and frankly, she was ready for whatever compromise was necessary. As she'd just told Kate—focus on the big picture. "Can I help in any way?"

"My parents asked me to come over for dinner tomorrow night. I was wondering if you'd like to join me."

Ellie could only imagine what her face had to look like because Jordan laughed softly. "Too soon?"

"No! I mean...no, I'm just surprised, that's all. I'd love to. They know you're bringing someone, right?" Then something else came to mind, and the words were out before Ellie could rethink them. "They're not expecting Bethany, are they?"

To her relief, Jordan shrugged off her inappropriate question. "I don't think so," she said. "If anything, Bethany had a hard time warming up to them and vice versa."

"So..." Ellie leaned back in her chair, hoping she wasn't getting ahead of herself. "Meeting the parents. That means exactly...what?"

"It means I missed you, and I'd really like to spend some time with you."

That was almost too good to be true.

"I'd like that too."

"Plus, if there's someone else around, there's not so much of a danger they'll ask about Darby." Jordan looked a little guilty at that. "I know, I'm sorry. This is not what you've been hoping for, and I don't blame you if you don't want to get into this. Forget I asked."

"Wait. I understand, I really do." In the wake of the attack she'd suffered, Ellie had gotten the concerned treatment from friends and colleagues. She appreciated all those offers, but when they came in bulk, they were simply too much. There was only so much words could do. Besides, there were some images you didn't want to burden the minds of loved ones with.

"I still want to go with you. I'm glad you asked." It might be a small step, but it was a step, the silver lining Ellie had been hoping for.

"Thank you." Jordan gave her a rueful smile. "I think I will have that drink now. I'll be right back."

Ellie watched her walk to the bar, feeling happy and proud, of herself, of Jordan. She didn't want to analyze the moment too much, simply hold on to that feeling.

Jordan brought a beer for herself and a glass of white wine for Ellie. As usual, she had paid attention.

Ellie thought back to the rocky start they'd had, when Jordan was still with Bethany and couldn't seem to let go, and Ellie had decided she didn't care, feeling justified in the aftermath of what happened to her. There were no more excuses, just two people taking responsibility and starting over. It felt right, just like it had in those moments when they had abandoned all responsibility.

"I heard you're keeping the house," she said. It wasn't like they could avoid any given subject connected to Darby in the long run, and maybe Jordan was okay with that, she'd wanted to talk, after all. "I'm sorry I never called after...I thought you needed space. I didn't mean to sulk or anything."

"I know you didn't—and you're right," Jordan ascertained. "I needed to sort out some things. Turns out you were right and going to the therapist out of obligation was a bad idea. I think Bethany knows that too. The house is another thing, and with Hobbs on the run, it's still pretty crazy. I want you to be sure about what you're getting yourself into. I guess meeting the parents is part of that, but don't worry, they are pretty nice people. Makes sense too since we are not related by blood."

It was on the tip of her tongue to ask, and Jordan seemed to sense that.

"I'll tell you sometime," she promised, taking Ellie's hand. The feeling was almost electric—time and traumatic events hadn't changed *that* between them. "People seem to be talking about me a lot these days, but no one tells me any gossip about you. What's going on in your life?"

If Ellie was honest, there hadn't been much other than waiting and hoping. She'd done her shifts, quietly listening to any sort of information she could get, up until this moment.

"God, I missed you. I'm not ashamed to admit that it's pretty much all that's been going on in my life," she said, and that was as honest as she could get. Maybe she could be brave too. "Would you like to stay over tonight?" She wanted to tread as carefully and respectfully as possible. At the same time, she couldn't help longing for the intimacy they'd once had. Ellie knew that they had their respective, different ways of dealing, but Bethany being out of the picture would make everything easier.

"I can't, not tonight. I have an early start tomorrow. Maybe tomorrow, would that be okay?" Jordan's answer was swift and devoid of complicated emotions, or so it seemed. If there was anything else going on under the surface, Ellie couldn't tell. There was still hope. That was all that mattered.

"Sure," Ellie said. "That's even better."

"It's a date." Jordan gave her that warm, sexy smile that had attracted her from day one.

It was clear to Ellie that all the talking necessary wasn't done yet, but they would get there.

Chapter Five

J ordan was lucky Ellie had bought the "early start" excuse—in fact, Ellie's apartment was closer to both their workplace, so she might have just as well followed the invitation. Staying over came with hopes and expectations, and if she could stall one more day, that's what she was going to do. Talking to Ellie felt good, even though they had barely touched the surface, let alone anything that was slithering underneath. Maybe it didn't need to be right away. It looked like Ellie had made up her mind. She was an adult. Even if she didn't know the whole story, it didn't mean they couldn't give it a try, did it?

Sitting up on the side of her bed as the day dawned, Jordan sighed. There were a few points she could make. She was notoriously bad at relationships. While she refused to believe in Bethany's interpretation, her living circumstances during the first twelve years of her life might have made an impact. On the other hand, she was aware of it now. She could do better, right?

She might need space, and have nightmares, but that was something Ellie understood. There was no more explanation to unearth, no excuse. This time, it was all her responsibility, a realization that was frightening in itself. With Bethany she'd felt crowded even though they hardly saw each other unless they were working on a case together. Jordan pulled away, cheated. The first time had been meaningless to all involved, but then she'd found someone she fell for, someone who genuinely cared for her. Failing her was not option.

Jordan got up. She'd been dressed for work for a while, waiting until it was time to go. The early start itself hadn't been an evasion. She was determined to make good time so she could show up at her parents' house early and not stay too long. It was better this way.

Once Ellie met Jack and Pauline, she'd have context for everything Jordan hadn't told her yet. As she drove to the department, Jordan switched her thoughts to work, yesterday's search.

TJ Pratt seemed to have told the truth, as much of an oxymoron as that was. He was put in protective custody. The CSU had found fingerprints to place Phil Hobbs in the trailer, and by any logic, still somewhere around.

Why take that risk? He knew his chances of getting away would have been best in the first few hours. She didn't really think Pratt's theory was sound. A man like Hobbs would have nothing but contempt for the likes of Pratt or her birthparents—he would use them while he could, but in no way involve them in a more elaborate plot. Smart, scary psychopaths were loners and trusted no one—that's why they could get away with what they did for so long.

If Hobbs had decided to stay in the area, he had a reason, and that worried her.

At the department, she caught Henderson heading for the interview rooms, wondering what she'd missed.

"Hey, Derek, wait. Did something happen at the safe house?"

He looked surprised. "Why do you think that? I just have this interview to do. I don't really need you for it."

If she'd been suspicious before, this confirmed Jordan's worries that something was off. "What aren't you telling me? Come on. This is my case too."

He sighed and stopped walking, leaned against the wall in the hallway instead. "Let me do this, okay? We won't be able to keep Pratt in this place forever. If Hobbs is up to something like Pratt says, maybe some of his old associates have an idea, especially when Hobbs threatened them in the past."

She felt the blood drain from her face before he added, "I asked James and Kathryn Larson to come in this morning."

"Come on, I told you he's lying—or, at least, exaggerating."

"You believed that Hobbs was threatening him."

"Yeah, for that we have proof, sort of. They all used to hang out together and get high, fine, but Hobbs moved on to bigger things. Jim and Kathryn are—" She broke off the sentence, not sure how to come up with anything that wouldn't make her look bad. "I don't buy it. We are wasting time with them."

"I don't think so, and neither does the lieutenant. Like I said, you don't need to be in there."

Jordan had no idea why this was hitting her this hard, other than the fact that she was off her game already. Her past was something she had kept as hidden as possible from her colleagues. As far as they were concerned, her parents were Jack and Pauline, the friendly unassuming couple. She couldn't deal with the sympathy—or worse, pity—she had gotten from classmates back then. Especially now.

"I want to watch," she said.

Maybe it would be okay. It was unlikely they knew anything about Hobbs. They would walk out of this place, and everyone, including Jordan, would forget they'd ever been here.

Derek gave her a long considering look. She held his gaze.

"That's your idea of fun on a day off?"

"You know as well as I do that I can't sit around at home as long as Hobbs is out there. I'm having dinner at my parents' tonight if that makes you feel better. My real parents."

"That's something," he admitted. "All right. Let's get this done."

They walked the last few steps to the door in silence.

"Derek."

His hand already on the handle, he let go and turned around, probably hoping she'd changed her mind.

"Just remember, that's not me." *A victim of circumstances, that is, with Darby, and born to the wrong people.* As cryptic as those words sounded, he seemed to understand what Jordan meant. He laid a hand on her arm, briefly, and opened the door. For the first time in twenty-something years, Jordan laid eyes on the people she'd spent the first twelve years of her life with.

Detective Maria Doss was already in the room, introducing Derek to the couple.

"Thank you both for coming in," Derek said. "This won't take long."

"I still don't know why you asked us to come. We did nothing wrong," Kathryn Larson said defiantly, wringing her hands in her lap. "Shouldn't there be a lawyer present?"

Her husband James nodded. "We know our rights."

I bet you do by now. They were both in their mid-fifties, Jordan realized with a pang of an unwanted emotion. She had a case to solve, nothing more or less. There was no time to explore that tricky personal connection to these two people who looked significantly older than their age, years of drug and alcohol abuse taking their toll.

"We just need to ask you a few questions," Derek assured them. Doss stood leaning against the wall, arms crossed over her chest, looking pensive.

"Yeah, sure," Kathryn mumbled. "That's what they always say."

"You know a TJ Pratt?" Derek asked.

The couple shared a surprised look, then James answered. "We sure do. He lives in the trailer park. We've seen him around. No one likes him very much though. There's something off about him."

Kathryn sat, staring at her hands in her lap silently.

Jordan shook her head. She had known this would get them nothing. Besides, it was hard to buy the righteous indignation from two people who didn't have a care in the world except themselves. Thinking about those parties, the noise, the unbearably loud music and the smells gave her a headache. Her body remembered. In the cramped trailer, there hadn't been much space to get away from it all. In the summer, she'd always found places to hide away. In the winter, it wasn't so easy.

Malicious laughter.

Maybe that had happened in the basement of Jonathan Darby's home instead.

"What do you mean?" Doss followed up.

"Well...he would hit on the women, if they said no, he didn't take that too well. We were glad when he was gone. I don't know who he paid off in prison, but everyone was surprised when he got out. Fooled everyone, and now he's back. Doesn't surprise me though that you're looking at him."

"He did serve his time, though, unlike Hobbs...Have you heard from him lately?" Derek asked. "According to Pratt, you were close at some point."

"Hey, hey, hey," James protested, "don't go there, pal, okay?"

On the other side of the glass, Jordan cringed. She was aware of Derek's concerned glance.

"You're not saying we helped him? We didn't. We live a fairly peaceful life. We don't have much, but it's okay. We stay away from people like them. Seriously bad mojo. Can we go now?"

"Don't worry, we're not accusing you of anything," Doss spoke up. She sat down across from the couple. "Pratt specifically mentioned your names. He thought that Hobbs might seek revenge for when you refused to be his accomplices in a bank robbery."

Kathryn shook her head. "Hobbs?" she said with high-pitched laughter. "He couldn't get his head out of his ass, what makes you think he could rob a bank without getting caught right away? Frankly, we're stunned he's still out there. He wouldn't be if it wasn't for Pratt, that much is for sure. Pratt always meant trouble. Killed one of the neighbors' goats once. He ratted us out to child services, so you can believe us, we have no reason to cover for him."

Jordan tensed at the first hint of the connection she had with the two people in the interrogation room, unwanted, unwelcome. She wished Pratt could have turned on them sooner. Twelve was old enough to have a lot of memories, and confusion. Jordan had no intention whatsoever of catching up, but the sight of them, all self-righteous and indignant—because it was always about them, right?—troubled her.

Her own blood. What did that make her? Could you escape your biological fate, or would she end up being that kind of irresponsible, selfish person who didn't give a damn about how anyone else felt? Bethany might say she was already there. Maybe she shouldn't have left couples' therapy, tried harder. In her heart, Jordan knew the outcome would have been the same eventually—because of her own selfishness or the fact that she and Bethany had never been a good match to begin with, it was hard to say.

"Do you have any idea where Hobbs might go, anyone he could contact, friends in common with Pratt?" Derek continued.

James Larson shrugged. "I could give you a couple of names, guys they used to hang with, but we have no idea where they are now. That was all a long time ago."

"We'll start with that," Doss said. "Your help is much appreciated."

She wrote down the names while Jordan watched the woman who had given birth to her, fidget in her chair. Although she had grown up less than thirty miles from the much-hated surroundings of her childhood, they had never tried to find her. Pratt's "betrayal" couldn't weigh so hard on them—what a sad irony that he had a hand in Jordan getting out.

There was a question on her mind, something she would have already asked if those people were any other witnesses. Jordan made a step forward. Her hand on the door handle, she hesitated. They didn't care. There was still a small risk. Jordan took a deep breath and opened the door.

"Detective Henderson? A minute?" The Larsons didn't even look at her.

"Excuse me for a moment," he said and joined Jordan in the observation area.

"Get her alone. Remember what he said about Pratt hitting on the women in the trailer park? I bet she was one of them. Look at her. She might be scared, or maybe she had an affair with him, either way he might have contacted her. Don't tell me you don't see it too," she added, not wanting to risk Derek thinking her theory sprang solely from the personal connection. "She's hiding something."

"It's possible. Okay, let's find out."

Derek asked Detective Doss outside and laid out Jordan's theory for her. Jordan breathed a sigh of relief when her colleagues didn't seem to think she was overreacting. They decided that Doss would do the follow-up questions, and they both went back into the room.

Alone again, Jordan leaned against the cool glass, trying to get a handle on the vicious headache. She didn't need a shrink to tell her what it meant.

"Mr. and Mrs. Larson, thank you for your time," Derek said. "Mr. Larson, would you please come with me? Mrs. Larson...Could you stay another moment with Detective Doss? I'll get you a coffee."

"Is there anything wrong?"

"Pratt alleged that you might be in danger from Phil Hobbs," Doss told her. "We are taking this very seriously. Please, Mrs. Larson."

Kathryn's demeanor changed when the two men left the room from nervous to defiant and angry. "What do you want? We already told you everything, and I'm not sure you even listened to us. It's TJ you should be looking at. It's always the same with you guys."

"Hobbs seriously injured a guard during his escape and held a woman hostage. We don't want to take any chances."

Her headache was intensifying. Jordan wasn't sure what she had expected, but the way James walked right past her, with no sign of recognition, was beyond sobering. Hell, this was what she wanted, distance, have the two of them out of her life. She couldn't have it both ways.

"Has either Pratt or Hobbs contacted you recently?" Doss asked softly. "It's okay. Your husband can't hear you."

Kathryn Larson clutched the paper cup so tightly coffee sloshed over the rim. She didn't seem to notice. With dread, Jordan recognized a familiar gesture.

"About Hobbs, I have no idea. I read that he escaped, but I have no idea how he could have pulled that off. TJ..." She swallowed hard. "He stopped by...just for a cigarette, he said," Kathryn finally said. "I know, you think it's strange I would even talk to him, after all, we nearly went to prison because of him—I thought he wanted to make amends. Sure, he did some bad things, but hasn't everyone? That was before all the crap with Hobbs went down, I swear I didn't know."

"You had a cigarette together, talked...about what?"

"About our daughter. TJ didn't find out until she was a teenager, and he got so pissed he told on us. A few weeks ago, he said he would try to find her."

"...and what?"

"Kill her," Kathryn Larson said matter-of-factly.

"He said that to you, and you didn't think it would be something we should know?" Doss took a deep breath, casting a glance towards the two-way window.

She didn't need to worry about Jordan—this day felt completely surreal already, and Jordan had gone back to whatever strange state would help her not to crumble. At this point, she was experienced. Our daughter—and she'd thought she'd had bad luck with her birthparents before. Leery, creepy TJ Pratt. This was why he'd come back, to taunt her. He wasn't going to kill her, but he sure wasn't above playing those games. When they'd first visited him in the trailer, he knew.

No.

Apparently, Kathryn had adopted some of the same coping mechanism: Denial.

"Oh, come on, the guy said a lot of things for two reasons—either he wanted to scare you, or get into your pants. You said it yourself, he lied about Hobbs, why should I have taken him seriously? I don't know where she is. I thought he was bullshitting me. Again."

So, Kathryn had recently shared a cigarette and some conversation with TJ, a man she believed to have helped Hobbs escape, who allegedly killed a goat for no reason. The mere idea that all of it could be true, made Jordan sick to her stomach, more so with every moment it was sinking in.

"Did you try to warn your daughter then?"

"Do you ever listen? I believe TJ has his hands full if he helped Hobbs—which is the only thing that makes sense here."

"Is this woman for real?"

Jordan jumped. She hadn't even heard Derek come back in until he voiced his frustration.

"She'll say whatever. He's not coming after them, or me."

"How can you be so sure?" Derek asked.

"I know what you want to say, Derek. I'll make it easier on you. I can't be off the case. There I thought my family history sucked, go figure, it's even worse than I could have imagined."

"Let's have the lieutenant make that decision, and meanwhile, dig a little deeper into Pratt's history."

"Animal cruelty...You think he's been moving up in the world?" Jordan asked tiredly. "Like I need another serial killer in my life, my father no less."

"I know this is bad, but if anything, this means you're the poster child for overcoming bad family history. You have nothing in common with either of them."

"Except DNA." Jordan sighed, rubbing her temples which did nothing to alleviate her headache.

She could have sworn there was a hint of anger in his gaze when he looked back at Kathryn. *Don't*, she wanted to say. *Any emotion is wasted on these people—they won't change.* There was one thought on her mind, though, that she couldn't erase thinking about the woman that meant so little to her in the present.

You should have protected me.

"First of all, we need to check in at the safe house," she said. All of a sudden, that seemed like a priority, whether she believed Kathryn or not.

"Everything is fine," Officer Libby Marshall said. "Oh, could you tell Kate Jensen said to pick up the roses now. If she has time."

"Are you sure everything is okay over there?" Jordan asked. Derek, picking up on the sudden tension, looked over to her.

"No, but she can't forget. It's kind of urgent."

Libby sounded nervous which wouldn't be so unusual, as this was one of the bigger assignments for a rookie. Forget about that—something wasn't right.

"I'll tell her." Jordan covered the phone with her hand and mouthed to Derek, "Send units to the safe house. Right now." She hoped Ellie was somewhere on the other side of the city today, serving and protecting far from the mess this case was about to become.

"Okay, Libby, I'll pass it on. Kate will go right away, do you hear me? It'll only take a few minutes."

"Oh God, thank you."

"We'll be right there," Jordan promised.

"What are you doing?" Derek asked when she picked up her coat and keys and followed him outside the double doors. "Where do you think you're going?"

"Come on, we don't have time for this."

"That's right, and you know as well as I do that you shouldn't be anywhere near Pratt right now."

"You are not the boss of me!"

"That's right, but I am, so could someone tell me what's going on? Henderson? Carpenter?" Both of them spun around to come face to face with an impatient lieutenant.

"Sir, we need to go to the safe house right now. Something's off, and we just heard from the Larsons that Pratt might be the bigger threat after all. It could be his connections, not Hobbs' that got him out. We need to hurry."

"You go. Keep me updated."

"Will do. Thank you, sir." There was no time for gloating. Jordan was only grateful she was still on the case, even if it might not be for much longer.

Derek walked to his car in long angry strides, barely waited for her to fasten her seat belt before he hit the gas pedal.

"It's okay if you're mad at me. Just don't take it out on the car."

"Jesus, Jordan, I'm not mad at you. What if this was any other cop? You'd tell them the same!"

"Parental tests still pending. I'm not sure I'd take the word of a drug addict for the truth."

"Apparently she was right about something."

Jordan had nothing to answer to that, so she turned her attention away from Derek, listening to dispatch instead.

"You're aware that the moment we get back to the lieutenant, he will take you off the case? This is not about Pratt at all, is it?"

"I can do my job," she said angrily.

"We're all aware of that, but there are other cases. You could—"

They both froze at the voice crackling over the radio, with the rapid-fire staccato of someone relating a catastrophic situation. The officer was at the safe house, and he confirmed everyone's worst nightmare with the two words *"Officer down."*

Chapter Six

D erek made no further attempt to hold her back when they arrived at the scene. The remote location was filled with hectic but controlled activity. An ambulance was speeding away. When they got out of the car, the coroner arrived.

Every disturbing revelation, the confrontation with her past, the silly argument with Derek, all of it seemed irrelevant all of a sudden. The scene appeared unreal, the grim determination in the faces of their colleagues a thin layer over shock.

They found Sergeant Bristol in the hallway, his face ashen.

"Detectives." He nodded to them. "In here."

Most of the house was pretty non-descript, impersonal décor and furniture. The living area was chaotic, armchairs overturned, bullet holes in the walls.

Jordan forced herself to look at the body in the center of the room, lying in a pool of blood that had soaked the carpet and was already drying around the edges.

"Oh God." The words were out of her mouth before she could stop them. She knew they were some of Ellie's closest friends on the job, Kate McCarthy, Libby Marshall and Kate's fiancé, Jensen Baker. There would be no wedding now.

Baker had been an easygoing, happy-go-lucky kid, always friendly, the kind who did great connecting to people. Jordan didn't know his exact age, but he couldn't have been older than twenty-eight.

"Do we..." She cleared her throat. "Do we know what happened in here? I had Marshall on the phone less than twenty minutes ago."

Sergeant Bristol pointed to the holes in the wall. "Detective Cordova who was here with Marshall and Baker was unresponsive. They're on the way to the hospital."

"What about Marshall?" Jordan asked, her stomach clenching painfully with the overpowering smell of the blood.

"It was touch and go when they left," he said and sighed heavily. "Hobbs came for Pratt after all, and it looks like he brought reinforcement. We don't know how many yet. They took the officers' guns too."

The bad news just kept coming.

"We think Pratt might be the one who orchestrated all of this," Jordan told him. "And we went for it, gave him the perfect setup."

"No one knew for sure, there was nothing in his history to suggest this could happen," Derek reminded her. "Hobbs has the rap sheet to go with this kind of violence."

"Find them. Excuse me now," Sergeant Bristol said. "I have to contact Officer Baker's parents and go to the hospital after."

"Sergeant," Jordan called after him. "Does Officer McCarthy know?"

"Frankly, I'm not sure. I'll send someone after her, make sure she's okay."

Jordan nodded, thinking that it would be a long time before Kate would be anywhere near okay. She made a mental note to inquire for her after they were done processing the scene.

Ellie arrived in the company of Officer Casey Lyons, a fifteen-year veteran with the PD, fortunately after the coroner had left with the body. The sight of the bloodstained carpet was enough to make her pale though, and Jordan reached for her shoulder quickly.

"Hey," she said, wishing she could say anything that would be helpful to Ellie at this moment, coming up empty.

"So, it's true," Ellie said, her eyes wide, as if there had been any doubt until now. "We couldn't be here earlier. We were literally on the other side of town, with this burglary..."

"There's nothing you could have done. I'm so sorry."

"I can't believe this...I...I talked to him last night."

"I know." Jordan wished there weren't so many other people around, and she could just give in to the impulse and hold her close. On the other hand, neither of them would be comfortable with this kind of gesture in public. It had to wait. "Okay," she said, "I have to go back. We have to wait for the ME's preliminary report, and there's the footage from the security camera."

"Hobbs did this?" Ellie took a shuddering breath.

She was still too pale for Jordan's comfort. "We're not sure, but the video will hopefully tell us more." Jordan thought of Marshall's desperate attempt to send a message, too late. Roses for the wedding.

"Does Kate know?" Ellie asked anxiously, her eyes brimming with tears she barely held back.

"Bristol sent someone to check on her. I don't know. Look, why don't you come back with me? We need to talk."

The buzzing of her cell phone interrupted her. Jordan knew right away that the lieutenant calling her at this moment couldn't mean anything good.

"Carpenter, I want you back here and in my office."

"Henderson and I were just about to—"

"No, tell him he can wrap things up. I'll send Doss. It's you I need to talk to." Jordan disconnected the call, slightly stunned, asking herself how this day could possibly get any worse. It was a nightmare already, and there was no end to it anytime soon.

"Change of plans. It looks like you'll be working with Detective Doss," she said to her partner. "Ellie, I'm sorry, I need to go. I'll see you later." Jordan hoped it was enough to convey that later would entail whatever Ellie needed, food, alcohol, any comfort she could possibly give her. There was no need to say it out loud that family dinner was canceled. She'd have to call her parents too.

In the car, Jordan wiped her face in a quick angry gesture. There was no time for tears, and no reason to feel sorry for herself when she already knew what the lieutenant was going to say. Either way, with today's terrible loss, she had no reason to complain.

"I understand you were eager to get back to work, and everyone supported you. You thought it was not necessary to mention the death threats Pratt made against you?"

The lieutenant hardly ever yelled, but he did let his detectives know when they had screwed up, without any doubt.

"There were already a number of units on the scene when we arrived," Jordan offered, aware it would be far from enough to save her. On the other hand, if she stayed silent, she'd give him the wrong impression.

"You couldn't know that. In fact, it could have been a trap he laid out for you—"

"Oh please. I'm not important to every lowlife in this city." Jordan was well aware of the fact that she was treading on dangerous ground. "What do you suggest?" she asked.

"So glad you ask my opinion, Detective. I want you to go home."

"What do you mean? I can't—"

"Sure you can. This is the second of your days off you're spending here. Come back on Monday and help Waters with his caseload."

What he didn't say was that for the time being, Derek would be partnered with Detective Doss. Jordan bit her lip to hold in the retort. She wasn't happy with this arrangement, but at least he hadn't suggested she'd take a longer break.

"There'll be an officer at your house." He must have read something in her expression because he added, "Cut it out, Carpenter. We lost an officer today. I won't take any risk."

"I understand. Thank you, sir."

Dejected, Jordan walked back to her desk and sat behind her computer for a moment before she turned it off.

What had they overlooked? Had something horrible happened because *she* hadn't dared to take a closer look? Much as she hated it, Jordan had to admit that both the lieutenant and Derek had a point. She was much too close to all of this, not because she felt any ties to Jim and Kathryn Larson, but because she was uncomfortable and overwhelmed with everything that could be uncovered.

Still, it didn't seem right to take an evening off while every other cop was out there hunting Baker's murderers. She hadn't heard any news on Cordova, Marshall, or McCarthy.

Jordan picked up her cell phone to call Pauline and cancel dinner. It was early enough that she might even make it, but she didn't feel like company tonight. Not that kind of company anyway.

"I heard it on the radio," Pauline said, her tone soft and sympathetic. "Are you okay? Are you sure you don't want to come?"

"Another night. I'm sorry."

"That's fine, sweetie. Please call."

"I will. Bye." She ended the call, looking up to see the lieutenant standing in the doorway of his office, his disapproval showing. Jordan shrugged and got up from her chair to leave when Ellie walked in. She had changed into civilian clothes already.

She gave Jordan a tired smile. "I was hoping you'd still be here."

"I'm sorry I canceled dinner. You could still come over," Jordan said, lowering her voice. "I was sent home."

"I'd love to. I just wanted to go to the hospital first."

"Any news?"

Ellie shook her head.

"I'll come with you," Jordan decided.

Chapter Seven

T hey made the drive to the hospital in their respective cars, which was probably just as well. Ellie was afraid that the moment they'd be together with no one else around, she'd be tempted to let her guard down, to allow the wave of emotion she'd managed to hold back so far. Jordan might have her own issues, but Ellie felt safe with her. However, this wasn't about Ellie. She was grieving for a friend and colleague—she couldn't imagine how Kate had to feel. No, that wasn't right. She could, and that was the scary part.

They found Kate with a group of cops gathered in the waiting room together with Libby's family, exchanged greetings in hushed tones.

"I'm so sorry," Ellie said, struggling to keep her composure in front of her friend. Kate's face looked ashen. Her hands were trembling.

"Don't hug me," she warned. "I'll lose it." She pressed her lips together as if holding in a scream. Ellie *could* relate. She'd felt that way, constantly, during the search for Jordan—except they'd been lucky. Kate wasn't. She looked over to where Libby's parents sat in a corner, holding on to each other's hands.

"She's hanging in there," Kate answered her unspoken question. "Lost a lot of blood, but she's going to be okay." Her eyes welled up. "Oh God, Ellie, what am I going to do? I have to tell all these people there'll be no wedding, I don't even know—My sister's coming in today, I couldn't even reach her yet. I can't see her! I can't talk to anyone right now."

"We are here for you," Ellie said. "Whatever you need, we can help you."

The flash of doubt in Kate's expression didn't go unnoticed. Ellie couldn't blame her. Having someone to lean on was helpful, eventually, but there was part of dealing with a trauma that you had to go alone, no matter how well-meaning the people around you were.

The same went for her—or Jordan.

"I don't understand," Kate said, her voice small. "How could this happen? Why us?"

Ellie didn't have answers for her even though she'd had the same questions. *Bad shit happens randomly to good people?*

"We'll get him," she promised, "and he'll spend the rest of his sorry life behind bars."

Kate pondered that prospect for a moment. "Does that make it better? That Darby's behind bars, does it really make a difference for you?"

Jordan stood by the window with another officer. Ellie could tell from the minute change in her composure, a sudden tension, that she'd heard Kate's question.

"It helps," she said. "At least we know he can't hurt anyone else. When is your sister coming? Would you like me to call her?"

Kate shook her head as if trying to come up with an answer was too much at this moment. Ellie was hopeful though that she had come here, sought the companionship of colleagues who were just as shocked about the outcome of this night.

"Yes, maybe," Kate said finally. "Thank you."

"It's okay." Ellie made her decision in a split-second, stepped forward and embraced her friend, because Kate looked like she was going to crumble.

"It's not fair," she sobbed, and Ellie could only agree.

"You're right, it's not. I'm so sorry."

She held on tightly, for the moment forgetting everything except the friend who needed her comfort. Ellie wasn't sure how much time had passed until Kate calmed down from sheer exhaustion.

She flinched at the gentle touch of a hand on her shoulder.

Turning around, she faced Jordan who looked like she could use a hug too.

"Jordan. I was just going to make a call for Kate."

"Hang on a second."

The surgeon had arrived to talk to Libby's family.

Ellie left after getting the news, driving out to Jordan's in the pouring rain. Libby *had* lost a lot of blood, but she'd been lucky, all things considered. The bullet had missed any vital organs—wasn't that what they always said? It was good news though, a relief for everyone assembled. They were eager for her to wake up, also because she'd be the first to give an account of what happened at the safe house.

After Ellie had exchanged a few words with Kate's sister, Kate had been able to talk to her.

They would pick up the pieces, somehow.

Everything still felt unreal, Kate's despair, the people in the waiting room, the...blood. There had been blood on the floor of Jonathan Darby's basement as well. Ellie was jolted out of her dark musings when the driver behind her honked—the light had turned green. She'd better pay attention. An accident was the last thing she needed.

When she pulled into the driveway of Jordan's house, Jordan's car was already there, as well as another unmarked vehicle.

Ellie still had a hard time understanding some of the choices Jordan had made, buying this house out of the city, keeping it after Darby's true identity came to light. It wasn't up to her to judge, but she did wonder.

"You made it, good. Are you hungry?" Jordan asked after she closed the door behind Ellie. "I could offer you frozen pizza. We could order in, too, but as you can imagine, that takes a little longer around here. Oh, Ellie. I'm so sorry."

Ellie hadn't meant to start crying the moment Jordan pulled her close. She couldn't hold back the tears no matter how hard she tried, or the images. They'd hung out together pretty much from the first day at the academy, celebrated each other's successes and got each other through embarrassing rookie mistakes. They'd shared secrets, gossip, dreams, and aspirations.

The last time Ellie had been in a squad car with Jensen, she'd brushed him off because she'd been irritated with the lack of progress regarding her relationship with Jordan. She remembered Kate and Jensen, so excited about announcing their engagement they'd thrown rounds for everyone that night.

No more wedding.

After the attack, Ellie had tried hard to make sense of a senseless incident. She'd decided that she'd paid her dues, and that in some way, the universe owed her, had to give back for the safety and confidence she'd lost. She'd even gone as far as deciding that the universe owed her Jordan whom she'd lusted after the moment she'd first laid eyes on her—regardless of the fact that Jordan was still in a complicated, conflicted relationship with FBI profiler Bethany Roberts.

She wasn't so sure anymore that there could be any order, any justice to what the universe dished out. Kate was a widow before she had the chance to be a bride. Jordan had a lot to deal with as well.

Ellie pulled back before she'd fall asleep from the gentle touch of Jordan's hand brushing over her hair.

"Wow, I'm sorry. I meant to say hello first."

Jordan gave her a wistful smile. "It's been a horrible day. You're entitled."

Ellie accepted the tissue she handed her and wiped her face. "It's been horrible for everyone though."

"What have you heard?" As expected, Jordan made some distance, busying herself with filling two glasses of wine and putting the aforementioned pizza in the oven.

"Not much, just that they brought in...your parents this morning. I guess that's why the lieutenant took you off the case. I'm sorry."

Jordan returned to the couch with two glasses of red wine, handing one to Ellie. She sat next to her. "He had no choice," she said, resignation obvious in her tone. "I really would have loved to introduce you to Jack and Pauline before you ever heard of the Larsons—but it turns out the truth might even be worse. Kathryn Larson said she had an affair with Pratt, with consequences, obviously. She might be lying, but why would she? It's not exactly a great demonstration of character. Oh, and apparently, he threatened to kill me, but she's not sure how serious he was about that. This is why the boss wants me off the case. I should have told you all of this before I lured you all the way here."

"It's okay. There wasn't ever a moment when you had the time. I'm here now. I'm not going anywhere."

Maybe it wasn't the start either one of them had hoped for, but it was a start all the same. Under the circumstances, neither of them had anything on their mind but sleep, though it would be elusive. Ellie was grateful that they had each other to hold on to.

Chapter Eight

B oth Pratt and Hobbs continued to elude the police in spite of a widened search and a hotline that generated many tips, none of them helpful. Pratt's witness had quickly come around in the wake of the horrific news. Dean Johnson admitted Pratt had given him money to tell his story.

The Baker family, who had intended to come for an engagement, arrived in town for their son's funeral instead.

The rain was coming down in sheets, fitting, Jordan surmised. Was it selfish to think that, not so long ago, she'd come close to having her own funeral? Probably. Officer McCarthy, Kate, stood with her own family. Libby Marshall and Cordova were still in the hospital. She would be released within the next few days whereas the detective was looking at a longer stay. At least, both their statements had helped piece together the timeline of the attack. Neither of them had seen Hobbs at the scene, but the men who barged in shooting certainly knew Pratt.

Ellie sat with Jordan in church but joined other officers at the cemetery.

It was also selfish, and highly inappropriate to think of Ellie sleeping in her arms the night after the shooting, a memory that was surprisingly calming. Jordan had come clean about her family, but that didn't mean every obstacle was out of the way. She was aware that Ellie might have other questions she hadn't dared to voice yet. She was also a police officer, able to piece the evidence together.

Evidence for what?

Jordan flinched at the sound of a familiar voice.

"I wish I could have seen you again under different circumstances." Bethany sighed. "Yet here we are."

"Why are *you* here?" Jordan bit her lip. She had answered without thinking, taking the bait as usual. She dared a sideways look. Bethany looked very much put together among the sea of mourners sheltered by black and dark blue umbrellas. Jordan had no idea what her connection to the Baker family was, if there was any.

"I work with the older sister," Bethany informed her patiently. "The Bakers are a third-generation law enforcement family. Such a shame," she added, as if that made a difference to the tragedy, or the family's grief. "I heard you took some time off. That's good."

Jordan hadn't sought out Bethany's blessing, but given the circumstances, she held back the clarification. Her continued silence wasn't enough of a hint for her ex-lover.

"I also heard...other things. How are you doing?"

"Okay," Jordan answered curtly. She had no idea how Bethany managed to convince people she should be in the loop about these things, but it was no surprise that she did have a way of making it happen. It wouldn't be the first time.

"Baby. You don't have to be that way with me."

It was out of respect for Jensen Baker that Jordan didn't yell at her, though she wanted to.

"I'm sorry," she said, struggling to keep her voice quiet. "I don't know any polite way to say it—I need you to stay out of my life from now on. No more going behind my back for any information or gossip that's not job-related."

"I still care about you."

"Stop it, Bethany, please. I'm with someone else now."

"Harding doesn't know you like I do."

"You think? I told her about my parents, and everything nasty that's come out in the past few days."

Bethany gave her a long look, her eyes widening slightly when she got confirmation of the implied question.

Yes, that too. I trust her enough to bring out all the garbage.

"That was quick," Bethany admitted. "Are you sure you two can handle that—you are both in a rough spot right now, so...Who knows what else you might remember? Anyway. She knows you don't have a habit of being faithful, so maybe she actually does have an idea of what she's in for."

"Really, here, at the funeral? That's pathetic even for you."

"It's not me you're angry at. It was never me."

"I wouldn't count on that." Jordan turned and walked away, the only way she could ever win an argument with Bethany.

❦

The atmosphere at the department was subdued, everyone still reeling from the impact of the recent events. The 911 call came in at 1:17 p.m., gunshots fired in an area that was infamous for gangs and drug-related crime. The officers on the scene reported one dead, a woman in her late twenties. Jordan prayed there wouldn't be another baby left behind—for the sake of the child and her wardrobe.

Detective Waters, her temporary new partner, wasn't much of a talker. Today, it was something that served Jordan well. She and Derek had grown close over the years, and maybe that made it easier to cross a line as well. After her confession to Ellie, she didn't need another deep conversation that left her vulnerable. Solid police work meant solid ground under her feet, and it was exactly what she needed now. Ellie had switched to the night shift this week, but she had agreed to come by at the end of it.

"Here we are," Waters announced the obvious as he parked on the curb, next to one of a group of grey blocks rising about ten stories each. A uniformed officer greeted them at the entrance.

"It's on the eighth floor," he said, "apartment 821. Mrs. Clayburn in 823 called the police. She heard arguing, a man's voice, then shots and someone running away. We've started canvassing the neighborhood, nothing so far."

"Elevator?" Jordan asked, and he shook his head. "Yeah, I figured. Thanks." She and Waters climbed the stairs in silence, story after story. She wasn't surprised that the only open door belonged to the apartment that was now a crime scene. Waters paused at the top of the stairs, catching his breath.

Jordan thought that all that extra time at the gym was paying off for her.

Gun violence wasn't uncommon in this part of town, but the similarities between the scenes were still disturbing. Another senseless death. It was getting to her. Maybe she should have taken more time off.

"One gunshot to the chest, shooter knew what they were doing," the medical examiner, kneeling next to the body, said.

The apartment was modestly furnished, no family photos to be seen anywhere. A professional hit? Gang-related?

There was a small desk in the corner of the room, unopened bills piled up, addressed to a Mara Lyman.

A search of the apartment turned up no further ID—the shooter had taken Mara's wallet with him. Probably not for riches inside, Jordan surmised, but something that could help identify the man Mara had been arguing with. An ex-boyfriend she wanted to leave? Sadly, that was a story that repeated itself over and over again.

"He didn't find this, though," Waters said as he came out of the bedroom, holding up a package containing a white powder in his gloved hand. "Gives us an idea what they were arguing about, even though no one but eighty-year-old Mrs. Clayburn heard anything."

"Maybe it wasn't hers," Jordan said.

"We'll see when we run the prints on the ceiling panel she hid it behind. There's more up there."

Jordan frowned. She didn't like that Waters made his conclusion so quickly, dismissing hers before she'd even voiced it.

"There's a lot of domestic violence in this area too. She could have been just...caught in the middle."

"Let's wait 'til we have all the information, so we can make informed guesses, all right? I know what you're thinking, but not all men are women-hating monsters. This looks all the way like an argument between two small-time drug dealers gone bad."

"A small-time drug dealer with excellent shooting skills."

"Exactly. Which doesn't help your theory about the angry boyfriend, does it?"

Aware of the medical examiner's curious looks, Jordan decided she didn't need to answer this question.

"Let's swing by Mrs. Clayburn and then see what else we can find on Mara," she said.

⁂

"She was a good girl." Mrs. Clayburn shook her head in sorrow. "Always quiet and polite. She worked two jobs, one as a janitor in a high school. She loved those kids, told me once she would have liked to be a teacher."

Jordan could tell what Waters was thinking—easy access to potential buyers.

"Do you know if she was seeing someone?"

"No, I would have known."

That made her cringe a bit, and grateful to live in a home that stood at a considerable distance from neighbors, no matter how friendly and well-meaning. "Are you sure? You said it was a man arguing with her before the shooting?"

"Yes..." Now she looked a little doubtful. "I'm sorry I can't tell you what they said. Everything went so quickly, and I don't hear very well..."

*Well, enough to be sure Mara Lyman didn't have a boyfriend...*Jordan wasn't willing to concede the theory of the vengeful ex yet.

"She was always by herself," Clayburn continued. "That's how I knew something couldn't be right when I heard the voices...and then the gunshot. I called the police right away." Her eyes welled up. "I'm so sorry. Maybe I should have done more..."

"You did everything right," Jordan interrupted her. "Thank you for your time, Mrs. Clayburn. If you remember anything else, please don't hesitate to call."

"What was that about?" Waters asked when they had left the apartment and walked down the stairs. Eight flights of stairs, again. Jordan had preferred the silence.

"We were done there, weren't we? She doesn't know anything else."

"Look," he said, halting so abruptly they nearly collided. "Pratt fooled all of us. What happened was not your fault."

"I never said it was, but thanks anyway."

He shrugged, but fortunately let the subject go, and they were back to blessed silence.

At the department, Jordan ran a check on Mara Lyman, who, on paper, was the good girl Clayburn had described, no parking tickets or unpaid bills. Jordan remembered the unopened letters in the apartment, mostly advertisements. Had Mara just come back from a trip? With someone as quiet and unassuming as the neighbor had described her, it wouldn't be too far-fetched to think no one would notice if she was away for a short while—doing what?

Jordan decided it was early enough to run by the school that had been one of Mara's employers. Waters didn't object. He didn't seem to want to join her either, so she suppressed a sigh and left. She missed Derek already.

To her surprise, there were a couple of squad cars already parked in front of the school. She hadn't expected to see Casey and Ellie either.

"You're late to the party," Casey observed. "Two kids caught with a locker full of heroin. We were just about to give them a ride downtown." She shook her head, her expression somber. "Sixteen, for God's sake."

"They have bigger problems. We found their janitor shot dead, with a kilo of heroin hidden in the ceiling."

"Yup, high school is not what it used to be," Casey scoffed. "Can you imagine what's next?"

Unfortunately, Jordan could imagine all too well. When Child Protective Services got her out of that trailer, they had saved her life in so many ways, even though at the time, she'd had a difficult time seeing it. Relief, guilt, anger, it was all part of the realization that the people who had brought her into the world weren't fit to take care of her the way they should have.

"Not sure I want to," she said. "I have to go find the principal now. I'll check in with you later."

"Why don't you let me know when you're back, and we can bring you up to date?"

That elicited a small smile from Ellie. Jordan thought it was a good idea too. "All right then. I'll see you later."

Under the looks of curious students, she headed for the principal's office where she knocked on the door and entered the room. A weary-looking woman got up from behind her desk, making a dismissive gesture when Jordan started to identify herself.

"That's fine. I'm Principal Allen, as you probably already know. Just please tell me it's not something worse."

Jordan winced. "I'm afraid it might be. About Mara Lyman, your janitor..."

Allen gave her a bleak look. "What about Mara? I thought this was about the drugs...Wait, you're not telling me she was involved? The drugs were uncovered in a random search, and we notified the police right away. Ms. Lyman has been sick for a while. We had to name a replacement."

"Mrs. Allen, I'm sorry to tell you, Mara Lyman was found dead earlier today."

The principal stared at her in shocked disbelief. "What's going on? First the drugs, now Mara..."

Yeah. I could use a change of setting too, Jordan thought tiredly. "You said she was sick. Can you tell me what exactly...?"

"Back problems, I think." Allen opened a drawer and took out a folder, leafing through it. "She was going to get surgery for it, but meanwhile she was in so much pain she couldn't work."

"To your knowledge, did she have a drug problem?"

"Why would you say that?" Allen asked with indignation. "She was a hard worker, completely reliable until her health problems started." She shook her head, wiping a hand over her face. "God, what a day. It's all so unreal."

"I understand this is difficult, but do you have any idea about Ms. Lyman's personal life?"

"Hell if anyone does. She kept to herself, did her work, only talked if she had to. This is a terrible coincidence, Detective."

Jordan had a hard time believing that, but at this point, she didn't need to make the woman's day any worse.

Chapter Nine

"A secret admirer?" Casey asked, amused, when Ellie's cell phone buzzed for the third time during the short drive.

"Hell if I know. Guy keeps sending me texts. I should tell him he's got the wrong girl." She'd gotten a couple of messages before, "I miss you," "I wish you were with me tonight," clearly a wrong number, but she didn't have the time or inclination to engage with the sender. Too many mixed emotions about this day, trying to keep it together because Kate couldn't do it any longer. With her and Libby out, Ellie was, like a couple of her colleagues, working an extra shift.

On the bright side, they'd run into Jordan at the school, and she'd get to talk to her a bit more later, hopefully spend some time after her second shift. Ellie decided she wouldn't ask about the conversation with Bethany at the funeral unless Jordan brought it up. She wasn't surprised Bethany was still the overly present ex-girlfriend, under the circumstances. Ellie couldn't even blame her much, though she wished that after the failed couples' therapy, Bethany would get the hint and move on just as Jordan had.

"Well, first we'll have a talk with these gentlemen," Casey said with regard to the scowling teens in the backseat, "and then you can report to Detective Carpenter. Maybe he'll get the message eventually, if you keep ignoring him."

"Let's hope."

"You can't interrogate me without my parents present," one of the students, Julian Grant, piped up. It was the first time he had spoken since the arrest. "We have the right to a lawyer."

"We'll call your parents, don't worry," Casey said, shaking her head.

His friend Jess didn't seem too happy about that prospect. "Can't you just let us go? We have nothing to do with the drugs. Someone set us up."

"Shut your mouth, stupid," Julian berated him. "Don't say anything until the lawyer is here. Don't you ever watch TV?"

Ellie and Casey shared a bemused look. Ellie assumed her colleague was just as grateful as she was for this little distraction on an otherwise dire day. With Hobbs and Pratt still on the run and the images of this morning still vivid on her mind, it didn't last long.

After booking, they took the students to separate rooms. As predicted, Julian's parents announced they would bring their lawyer. Jess's mother, on the other hand, sounded terrified over the phone. There wasn't much of a window.

Casey sat down with Julian, while Ellie entered the room where Jess was nervously wringing his hands in his lap. His mother hadn't talked about a lawyer.

"Julian said I'm not supposed to talk to you," he said defiantly.

"Julian's your friend?"

"What's it to you?"

Ellie shrugged. "Nothing, really." She paused for a moment. "Your mom will be here in a bit. Julian's parents talked about a lawyer...Do you think he will represent you too, or do you have one of your own?"

"Why?" Despite his suspicious stare, she could sense his uncertainty. There was something odd about the pair. A quick check of addresses had told her that both kids lived in very different neighborhoods. "If I can't afford a lawyer, you have to get me one, you told me so earlier. I won't need any, because I swear, someone put the drugs in my locker. I sure as hell would like to know who because the asshole got me expelled."

"Yeah, about that."

Ellie noticed him perking up briefly before he fell back into his earlier slump. "That's a lot of heroin. If you have any idea who did this, if you could help us, maybe we could put in a good word with the principal?"

"I have no idea who did it. Stop trying."

"Okay. Let's wait for your mom, then."

There was a knock on the door before it opened, and Casey peered inside. "Officer Harding?"

"Excuse me," she told the boy and stepped outside with the senior officer and narcotics detective Brannon.

"Grant's parents are here with the lawyer. If we charge him, he's likely to be out on bail tomorrow. How's it going in here?"

"He's scared," Ellie said. "I think he knows something."

"Mom's on her way. Scare him a bit more," Brannon advised.

Casey nodded in agreement. "No one had access to their lockers but these boys and the school authorities. He has to understand he's in trouble. When you're done here, go find Carpenter and see if she needs anything."

"Will do," Ellie said before she went back inside.

"So, Jess, looks like you and Julian will be here for a while. When the results for the fingerprints come in, you'll be charged and...Well, maybe one of you will make bail. I assume Julian will take the easy way out if he can, but I could be wrong. He's your friend after all. You trust him to have your back."

Silence.

Ellie was beginning to ask herself if her approach would lead to anything, but then he said, "Why would only one of us get bail? Doesn't matter if the parents are paying for a lawyer."

"True, but if one of you is cooperating, they are likely to get a better deal. I guess you don't have anything to worry about."

"Fuck, this is not how this was supposed to happen! I didn't want anything to do with this shit." He raked a hand through his hair in a nervous gesture.

"I'll try to help you best I can," Ellie promised, leaning back in her chair. "Tell me everything you know."

"I didn't know it was drugs, at first. Julian only said he owed someone money, and in return he had to store a package for a few days. He asked for my combination, I gave it to him. Damn it!"

"Did he say who he owed the money to?"

"Some guy named Carl. That's all I know. You have to believe me!"

"That was the first time Julian asked you to do this?"

He nodded.

"If there's anything else you can remember, you need to tell us. I believe Julian has gotten involved with some dangerous people. They'll want not only their money back, but those drugs too."

The door opened again, and a woman in her early forties came rushing in, Detective Brannon behind her.

"Jess, what the hell is going on?"

"Mom! I did nothing. I'm going to get a lawyer, and they'll get me out of here."

"My colleague will just have a few more questions," Ellie said.

In the other room, Julian Grant, after conferring with his lawyer, had considered his options, though he was telling a slightly different story to Casey and Brannon.

"Do I look like I need money? Jess here is the one who always gets into trouble. He said he'd get us some weed for a party. There was never ever talk about heroin, but I saw him talking to a guy at school."

"What guy?" Casey was rapidly losing patience with him switching gears again, her only consolation that this might actually lead to something. "Someone who works at the school?"

Grant shook his head. "Never seen him before. He was hanging out near the janitor's office—that was a while ago. Jess later told me that he's the one selling the stuff. I didn't ask until Jess turned up with a huge package of heroin he needed to guard for a few days. Hey, I don't do that kind of stuff, and I believe it's even a bit too hot for Jess, but man, he was scared shitless. The guy said if he didn't do it, he was going to send someone to beat him up."

"You ever heard a name mentioned?"

"Carl," Julian Grant said without hesitation. "I never got a last name. You see, I don't usually hang out with kids like Jess. They're bad news, and here I am, looking at possession charges."

"I'm sure the officer will take into consideration that you're coming clean about your mistake and regret it," the lawyer said.

Casey had a hard time keeping in the sigh when she imagined how many paychecks of hers the man's suit would be worth. "I'd really like to know what the game plan is. Since there's still no DA present, I don't assume you intend to charge my client? After all, the heroin is not his, and all he did was help a friend in need."

Casey was certain that the truth was a little more complicated than that, but unfortunately, one of the boys had more means and opportunity to spin said truth to his advantage.

"Just one more thing," she said. "When that guy used to hang around the school, was Ms. Lyman still working there?"

"The janitor? I think so, but I don't think she would have gone anywhere near him," Julian surmised. "She was afraid of her own shadow, that lady."

"What do you want to bet the drugs in those lockers were related to the ones you found in Lyman's apartment? It can't be a coincidence."

"I agree," Jordan said as she and Ellie sat at her desk for the update Casey had promised her. "Looks like neither of them is telling the whole truth either. With this amount of drugs, 'Carl' can't be one of the new kids on the block. Someone's bound to have heard about it. I think it's time I reach out to a CI of mine."

"I can't wait until I can say those words," Ellie said, prompting an indulgent smile from Jordan. "What do you think was Lyman's role in all this?"

"I'm so glad you ask." Jordan sighed. "Waters thinks it was some kind of turf war. Single woman, cautious to the point of paranoid, that tells me another story."

"You have the autopsy report yet?"

"No. It's a whole lot of waiting," Jordan said, her frustration showing.

"It's been a long day already," Ellie reminded her gently.

"No kidding. I thought you were working nights?"

"Apparently I'm working night and day at the moment." Not that there was anything funny about it. "With Kate and Libby on leave, we were a bit short-staffed today. From tomorrow, it'll be nights only for a while."

"How about you come by later and I'll make you breakfast?"

"I'd love—" Ellie jumped when her cell phone buzzed again. "For Pete's sake!"

"You need to get that?"

"Not really. Some guy with a wrong number. I really need to send him a text back sometime soon. Okay, where were we?"

"Breakfast."

"I would say, 'get a room,' but unfortunately, I still need Harding for a few more hours," Casey who had joined them, commented. "How about we get out and grab a bite to eat first?"

"Sure. You're paying?"

"Look at you, dinner and breakfast all taken care of. Sneaky."

It was with a strange mix of emotions that Ellie followed her after saying goodbye to Jordan. The fact that they'd been to a funeral this morning seemed far away and unreal, making her feel both relieved and guilty. Everyone working here, no matter how busy, was feeling the shock waves of this brutal event. The high tension wouldn't recede anytime soon, not until Pratt and Hobbs were arrested.

The night turned out to be fairly quiet. Ellie wasn't sure whether she should be grateful about it, when there was so much on her mind, and she was trying hard not to go back to the room in the safe house with the blood-stained carpet, or the morning at the funeral.

If she had a hard time dealing with this drastically altered reality, how much worse was it for Kate—and Libby and the other detective, who had survived the ambush?

Inevitably, this line of thought brought her to the fact that she had come close to losing a loved one to a violent crime. Not that she and Jordan had talked about love, because that would have been inappropriate at the time, but there was the potential...She wanted to believe, that after all these traumatic events, they still had the chance to pick up the pieces and move on.

Truth be told, there wasn't much else at the moment that kept her going.

"I know it's hard to believe that, but it's not always that way," Casey said. Ellie assumed it was easy to guess her thoughts these days, the attack, Darby targeting Jordan, and now the hunt for the fugitives...Some of her enthusiasm about being a cop, eventually becoming a detective, had vanished. Ellie wasn't sure if she'd ever get it back completely.

"I know," she said. "It's been a few horrible months, and I shouldn't complain when I wasn't the one..."

"Everyone understands. Baker was a good kid," Casey said. "I hope McCarthy will find a way to get over this."

"Yeah, me too." Ellie wiped at the corner of her eye. "You're trying to make me cry?"

"Not on purpose. I'm just saying that if you find something good, it's always a good idea to hold on, no matter what anyone else says."

"That's good advice. I think I'll take it, even it's unusually philosophical for you."

"Night shift. Brings out the best in people. Unfortunately, not all of us," Casey added when the dispatcher's voice came over the scanner, alerting them of a man trying to break into a building.

"14th street, that's the women's shelter," Ellie said.

"Yeah." Casey's expression was grim. "I don't think he just meant to say hello."

They approached the house cautiously, having no information yet as to whether the man, who was banging on doors and windows, threatening his wife, had a weapon or not. Linda Enders, the woman who ran the house, had given them a name: Rowan Walker. When they got out of the car, they could already hear him yelling.

"You come out right now! They're brainwashing you here. I won't let that happen!"

"How very convincing," Casey scoffed. "You go in the back in case he decides to run."

"He sounds pretty drunk. I don't think he'll run far."

There was a loud noise, and then the sound of glass breaking, sending them both running in the direction of the sounds.

"Police! Step away from the window!" Casey yelled. The man turned around obediently, staring at her as if dumbfounded that someone was trying to stop him.

"The police? I can't believe the bitch called the cops on me." He dropped the baseball bat he was holding and raised his hands, came walking towards them. "Hey, don't shoot, Ma'am. I'm a law-abiding citizen."

"I'm sorry, breaking into a house is not in the definition of law-abiding, Mr. Walker. Please come with us."

Walker spun around and ran towards the backyard.

"You're younger," Casey said. "Go." Ellie hadn't expected anything else. As she'd hoped, the intruder wasn't too fast, but he still made it over the fence that shielded the yard, thanks to a crate. Ellie followed him, almost safely on the other side when she slipped and fell face-first into a puddle. There was no time to curse or feel sorry for herself, so she gave chase for another block until the man rounded a corner and almost collided with Casey.

"Stop it right here—and don't call me Ma'am," she said, picking up her cuffs and fastening them around his wrists, before giving Ellie the once over. "When it rains it pours, huh?"

Ellie could only agree.

Chapter Ten

T hey met at the usual coffee shop. Darla had the hood of her red shirt pulled up, her shoulders hunched against the light rain. At this moment, she looked barely eighteen, though Jordan was well aware that this was not the case. Sacrifices, compromises, it was the same for all of them.

Darla had a sweet tooth, so Jordan knew to put a caramel latte and a brownie in front of her before they'd even started talking.

"What do you need?" Darla asked, a gleam in her eyes as she took in the sweet treats. "I'm sorry about that cop, by the way."

"Thanks. There's been an awful lot of heroin turning up in strange places lately."

"Is there ever a good place for heroin to turn up?" Darla asked sarcastically.

"Come on." Even though Jordan agreed with her, she hadn't come for idle chitchat. "A guy named Carl has been mentioned," she said. "Hanging around high schools. You hear anything about him?"

"Carl...I'm not sure."

"Darla, I need you on this."

"I'm trying, all right? Everyone's talking about Hobbs and how the police are doing a not-so-great job finding him."

Jordan shook her head. "I already regret this. Maybe we should call it a night." She still had some grocery shopping to do as well, for the breakfast she'd promised Ellie.

"Wait. I've seen someone—not Carl, his name is...Bud, I think. Yes, that's it. Big, scary guy, came to town a few months ago. Heroin, guns, he does a bit of everything."

"The locals just let him do that on their turf?" Jordan asked, doubtful about this story.

Darla shrugged. "He's got connections, I suppose."

"Where do I find him?"

"Whoa, lady, slow down a bit, it doesn't work that way. I saw him once at the *Pit*. You have to wait and let me see if I can find out something more. You go in there without a plan, you get me and yourself killed. Let's try not to do that."

"Fair enough," Jordan agreed. "I need a name, and you get me in there."

"Will do. You have to give me some time though."

"I don't have a lot of it. I've got a couple of high school kids with their lockers full of heroin, and a dead body in the morgue."

Jordan opened her wallet, counted off a few bills, then handed one to Darla. "The rest when you can get me to meet Bud. I'll come back with a plan, and no one's going to get killed, okay?"

"Works for me." Darla cast another longing glance at the bills that were not yet in her possession.

"There's something else. Does the name Mara Lyman ring a bell?"

"Should it?"

With a sigh, Jordan produced another bill. "Think. Was there someone else who might have stepped on Bud's, or anyone else's turf, that they might want to see go away?"

Darla shook her head. "Sorry, I never heard of her."

"Are you sure? She might go by another name as well, twenty-something..."

"That's the lady who got killed today? I saw her picture on TV in the mall. Never seen her before."

"All right. Thank you, Darla. I'll be in touch."

"I bet."

"Enjoy your coffee," Jordan said and got up. As she left the coffee shop, she felt lighter than she had all day. Something was finally moving into the right direction. With what Darla had told her, she couldn't entirely dismiss Waters's theory, but she didn't think it would hold in the long run. Mara Lyman was the victim here. With a little luck, she'd be able to prove it soon. Jordan had to grudgingly admit that it served her a lot more not to work on the Hobbs/Pratt case.

She'd share her findings with Waters, Brannon, and the lieutenant tomorrow. Now was the time to get some grocery shopping done to prepare breakfast for her girlfriend. Using this term for Ellie made her smile. *I guess we're there.* Time didn't stop. Their lives didn't stop. It was something to be grateful for.

Jordan stopped at the next store on the way, and a few minutes later, shook her head in amusement at the full cart. It might be a bit over the top for a breakfast in the middle of the week, when they would both have to go to work later that day, but after the barrage of catastrophic events she thought they both deserved a small time-out.

⟨⟩

Jordan managed a few hours of a surprisingly restful sleep before the alarm woke her. She'd set the table before going to bed and programmed the coffeemaker so everything would be ready by the time Ellie arrived.

When she did, she was still in uniform, greeting Jordan with a kiss, but warning her to keep a bit of a distance. "Would you mind if I took a shower first? I came here right away."

Jordan gently lifted a strand of her hair. "Is that mud?"

"Don't ask. It's been a long day and a long night. The coffee smells delicious though. I'll be quick."

"Sure. I waited with the food, because..." Jordan laughed, a little self-conscious. "I actually have no idea what you like for breakfast, so I bought a selection."

"I can't wait."

"Good. I'll get you some towels."

Minutes later, the sound of the shower came on. Jordan stood, leaning against the counter, a bit nervous and giddy alike at the thought of Ellie, naked, in her bathroom. For once, she didn't have to worry about painful conversations after a misstep—even if she'd brought that pain on herself, Jordan was aware. There was no need for secrecy anymore.

Maybe she should take another shower, too, a cold one. After the work hours Ellie had gotten behind her, some food and a soft bed would be all that was on her mind. Jordan could be patient as long as she knew they were on the same page and none of the recent revelations, no matter how dire, would make Ellie run. She was almost certain.

Ellie emerged from the bathroom with her hair still wet, but mud-free, wearing a white t-shirt and a green skirt. For a moment, Jordan found herself wandering back to the time when she'd first noticed her, sometime in the last year, always occupying that same table in the corner with her friends. A little later, stealing glances. It was hard to tell who had started it. The memory came with an almost forgotten sensation, its intensity startling.

"We thought it would be a slow night," Ellie said ruefully. "That was before we got the call about the guy taking a baseball bat to the window of a woman's shelter. Drunk as a skunk, but he still ran."

"Yeah. They always do. Um...sit down. I haven't cooked anything yet, because I wanted you to choose, but I can make you decent eggs with bacon. There's fruit, and Greek yoghurt, waffles..."

Ellie smiled before she stepped forward and kissed Jordan, the contact not quite as chaste as it had been earlier. Jordan framed her face with both hands but reminded herself to pull back when she still could.

"I'm sorry. I'm a terrible host."

"What if..." Ellie gave her a speculative look, enough to make her imagination run wild. Everything had been so difficult lately, not just in the past weeks, though those had easily been the worst in her life. Why couldn't it be easy for once? "What if we postponed breakfast for a bit? How soon do you have to go in?"

"I...I have a bit of time."

"Good," Ellie said. "I had so much coffee last night, I couldn't sleep right now anyway."

"You'd like to do something else, then?"

"God, I was afraid you'd never ask."

The feeling of giddiness remained, as one piece of clothing after the other fell to the floor on the way to the bedroom, in between heated kisses. It was still quick, and hot, but nothing compared to the rushed encounters they had to make do with when their relationship was still a secret affair. Jordan couldn't hold back the relieved sigh when they were finally skin to skin, limbs entwined in a messy lustful tangle. There was something good left in her life after all.

She couldn't believe she was this lucky, that Ellie had been patient enough for her to make up her mind, until she was brave enough to move on—from Bethany and from the memory of a serial killer's basement. The thought was fleeting though, vanishing quickly in the heat of the touch.

"I missed you. I missed this, so much," Ellie murmured, her fingers warm and confident, their explorations leaving room for nothing but perfect bliss. She placed soft kisses on Jordan's breasts, closing her mouth around a nipple, never stopping the rhythm of her fingers, until Jordan could no longer resist the tidal wave of sensation.

It occurred to her that this might be the first time in her adult life that she was in a relationship with someone who made her feel good about herself, in and outside of the bedroom.

She was more than willing to return the favor. "Just promise me one thing," she said when Ellie was sprawled underneath her, looking very comfortable, "don't fall asleep within the next few minutes. I know you came off a double shift, but it'd still make me doubt myself."

"You don't have to worry about that."

True to her word, a soft moan came over her lips the moment Jordan parted her thighs gently and started kissing her way downwards, slowly enough to make Ellie squirm. *I missed you too,* she thought, determined to demonstrate how much. Judging from the sounds above her, she was succeeding. Jordan brushed her fingers over Ellie's trembling thighs, and then she held on tight.

Jordan wasn't surprised when Ellie started crying the moment she pulled her into her arms.

They could have a time-out, but that didn't mean they could escape reality forever.

"I know. It's been crazy," she said, stroking a hand down Ellie's naked back.

"You could say that." Ellie gave her an embarrassed smile. "Look at me, doing that again. I'm so sorry."

"You're tired. It will be better with time." Jordan had to believe that those reassurances were more than idle hopes, otherwise, what would that mean for her?

"Yeah, I know it will be." Ellie snuggled close, her head on Jordan's chest. "So far, I managed not to do it at work, so I suppose that's a good thing. I hate to be so emotional when everyone else has their own problems to deal with."

"True. At least your father isn't a violent criminal on a killing spree...I'm sorry. I can't believe I said this. That's not what I meant. Just because everyone else is having a crappy time, it doesn't mean that you can't feel what you feel. I'm sure Kate and Libby understand that. I do." Jordan thought wryly she hadn't escaped unscathed from her long-term relationship with a psychiatrist—or maybe it was that she'd had to see too many shrinks lately. "That was a stupid thing to say though." She didn't know much about Ellie's family or the death of her parents, except that it happened a few years ago in a car accident.

"It's okay. Not everyone is lucky with their parents. I was." She sighed deeply. "It's not about that, really. A lot has happened in the past months. Please tell me it will be over at some point."

"It will be," Jordan promised, kissing her temple, relieved Ellie had given her an out on the subject. "Would you actually like the breakfast I promised you now?"

"Oh, please. I'm starving."

After they had collected their clothes and put them back on, Jordan poured coffee for both of them while she prepared eggs and bacon in a pan and put the rest of her purchases on the table.

"Wow. I know I said I was starving, but I'm not sure I can eat all of that."

"I had nothing in the fridge—and of course you're welcome to come by for breakfast all week if you like."

Ellie looked pleased at that, understanding that breakfast wasn't nearly all Jordan was talking about.

She had served the food and was about to sit down when something else came to mind. "Wait, what did you say before?"

"About starving? I admit that's a bit over the top, but all of this is delicious. I'll come back tomorrow morning if you'll have me."

"Yeah, no problem. About the intruder?"

"At the domestic violence shelter, yes. No priors. What do you mean?"

Jordan leaned in to kiss her cheek before she sat at the table. "See, Waters is giving me a hard time because he thinks Lyman might have been a dealer. Well, he thinks everyone in that neighborhood is a dealer. They all said Mara kept to herself and didn't date, but what if she was on the run from someone? Maybe she contacted one of the shelters in town. I'll be tied up all day, but you could ask around later."

"Absolutely," Ellie said, sitting up a bit straighter. "I will have to sleep first though."

"You do that. I have to go soon. Hopefully there'll be some reports on my desk. Would you like to crash here for a bit? I could give you a key, and you come back tomorrow morning." She realized she might have gone a bit fast when she saw the deer-in-the-headlights expression on Ellie's face. "I mean...as long as it's convenient for you. No pressure whatsoever."

"No, no, it's fine. I'll just go home to change later...and I guess I'll see you at the station."

"Thank you," Jordan said.

"Really, it's no problem. It's good to check in with the shelters once in a while anyway. They should know that we care."

"That's not what I meant. I mean...this." She hoped she didn't need to give any further clarification. Jordan wasn't sure she could.

"The world isn't ugly all of the time," Ellie said softly. "It's easy to forget that sometimes."

It turned out she had understood perfectly.

Jordan got up to pour them another coffee as Ellie's cell phone buzzed once more. She turned around, pot in hand, in time to see Ellie turn pale.

"What is it?" So much for a time-out.

"Nothing. I've been getting a lot of wrong numbers lately. It's annoying." Ellie sighed.

"Let me see? If they annoy you too much, we can do something about it, you know."

"No, it's not worth it. I'd really love to take you up on your offer though. There's not enough coffee in the world to keep me awake for much longer."

"That's fine, I need to go anyway. I'll see you at work."

"You will." Ellie gave her a smile that didn't quite reach her eyes, anticipating Jordan's reaction. "Don't worry. I'm tired. I'll need a little time to get used to changing shifts."

"Okay then. Sleep well," Jordan said, pulling her into an embrace before she let her go into the bedroom. She busied herself cleaning up in the kitchen before she got ready to leave, taking one last look into the bedroom where Ellie was indeed fast asleep. One day at a time. That was all they could do for now.

Chapter Eleven

E llie started her shift early so she could keep her promise to Jordan and drop by the shelter. It wasn't hard to tell that after the incident with Rowan Walker, the inhabitants had mixed emotions about the arrival of a uniformed officer. Their lives were already in upheaval—they didn't need any more of that. Ellie could sympathize. She was still torn between gratitude for the hopeful progress in her relationship with Jordan—and guilt, because she had taken this time when she could have been with her grieving friends.

Linda Enders had some interesting information for her. "Mara Lyman, no, the name doesn't ring a bell." Her eyes widened when Ellie showed her the picture. "That's her? I do know her. She came here a couple of years ago, but the hair and clothes were different. She was scared, didn't want to talk to anyone. She left one night without notice. Oh God. There's a reason you're asking me those questions."

Ellie nodded. With the stories Enders dealt with on a daily basis, she didn't need any more explanation.

"Her ex found her?"

"We don't know yet. Did she give you a name, did you file a report at the time?"

BARBARA WINKES

"Someone named Carl," Enders said. "She didn't give us much more information, said she didn't want to put anyone in danger."

"Thank you so much," Ellie said. "I'm sorry I couldn't bring you better news."

She excused herself to call Jordan who was appreciative of Ellie's report.

"Waters cannot tell me this is a coincidence. We got Julian's fingerprints on the heroin found in Lyman's apartment. It's the same quality. Now if only someone gave us a last name to this Carl guy. He seems to go by several names too."

"Maybe that's because he is new in town," Ellie surmised. "He was looking for Mara and finally found her here?"

"That's quite the grudge," Jordan said. "Thank you, in any case. Have a good shift. I'll see you later?"

"Yes, but I might not be able to stay long. I wanted to go check on Kate and Libby," she added quickly when the silence came with unmistakable questions. "I'm glad we..." Come to think of it, she really didn't need to say it out loud. "If you'd like to make me breakfast again, I won't say no."

"Good." Jordan laughed. "I bought so much food yesterday, it would likely go bad. At least, I'm starting to figure out what you like."

"You've known what I like for quite a while now." Ellie couldn't help it. The result was immediate. She felt excited that this intensity between them hadn't wavered now that they were both able to make choices.

When they first got together, it happened because Jordan wanted out of her relationship, and Ellie wanted to take back her life, any way she could, which included being with Jordan. Everything was different now. This time, their approach was a lot more mature, and Jonathan Darby and his sick fantasies had been nothing but a detour.

"Thanks. I'm glad to hear that. I'll see you tomorrow or sooner."

"Absolutely."

At the end of her shift, Ellie had received three more messages that convinced her she should be looking into the sender sometime soon.

Do you still think of that night? I do, all the time.

Why did you try to get away from me?

I still want you.

It was highly unlikely that these came from Rhonda. Ellie's only reminders of her ex were too big a check she paid every month for rent, and her hair color she couldn't seem to make a decision about.

After what happened to Jordan, and the latest tragedy in her circle of friends, she'd had little time to care about hair color—a subject for another day.

Leave me alone. You have the wrong person, she texted back to the unknown sender, almost expecting an instant reaction. She'd see if she could trace him, but that could wait.

After parking the squad car in the department's lot, she said goodnight to Casey and drove to Libby's apartment. To her surprise, she saw Kate's Mazda parked in front of the building. She walked up the stairs, her stomach in anxious knots.

Nothing would ever be the same. Kate opened the door to her and let her in silently.

"I am so sorry," Ellie blurted out. "I should have come by sooner, I just changed to night shifts, and there was so much to do...I'm sorry."

"It's okay." Kate pulled her into an embrace. "Libby and I decided that there was a limit to how many people we could stand to be around for a while. I'm glad you came though."

Libby was dressed, but she clearly bore the traces of her ordeal. There had been a fight before gunfire was exchanged. She was lucky to be alive, though it certainly wasn't easy to feel lucky in her situation. She accepted Ellie's careful hug.

"Just don't ask me how I feel," she said with a tone lighter than the circumstances would suggest. "That's still a big no."

"I can understand," Ellie said without thinking, then she shook her head. "I'm sorry. I know I can't say that, I have never..."

"Ellie," Kate interrupted her softly, a hand on Ellie's shoulder. "You've been through some bad stuff. We remember. It's not a competition."

"Oh my God." Her voice was suspiciously shaky. Ellie was determined not to lose it in front of her friends who had each been through an ordeal of their own, but those seemed idle hopes. "I swear I did not come here to cry to you. I'm sorry."

"That's okay." Libby squeezed her hand and motioned for her to sit down. "We were just talking about this. I know it looks bad right now, but we are determined to get through this, and we will. All of us."

"Yes," she said. "I'm all right with that."

While the exchange had been hopeful, it had also drained her, and by the time she slumped at Jordan's kitchen table once more, Ellie felt barely able to see straight any longer. She was curious though about the connections between Mara Lyman, the teens hiding the heroin, and the mysterious Carl.

"When we find him, we'll likely have our killer," Jordan said. "That would be at least something working out—job-wise, I mean. How are the girls doing?"

"Okay. Better than expected, I guess."

In the resulting silence, the sound of her cell phone seemed obscenely loud. "That's it," Ellie said with exasperation. "I thought it would be silly to waste department resources on this, but this guy is pissing me off. By now, he should know he's got the wrong number. Why does he keep texting?"

106

"Can I see?"

She handed Jordan her phone and watched her eyes widen as she scrolled through the messages of the past few days. "There are more than fifty," she said in disbelief. "Why didn't you report it sooner?"

Ellie shrugged. "I didn't think it was that bad...besides, I had a lot of other things on my mind."

Jordan looked a bit guilty at that, but she refused to let go of the subject. "That's a stalker. Did you notice anything unusual lately, someone following you?"

"No. Please. I'll look up the number and have someone take a look at him, if necessary, but frankly, all I want right now is a warm bed. I'd be grateful if it could be yours again, but I'm warning you. I'm not up for anything but sleep right now," she said with a wink.

"Ellie." Jordan sounded far more troubled than the situation required, Ellie thought. "This is bad. He's referring to the attack."

"Yeah, well, maybe they read about it in the paper. Clearly someone's having fun messing with me."

Her unease was growing. Ellie had wondered if she'd be paranoid to think of a connection, but Jordan seemed to assume the same thing.

"I know I probably should have taken it more seriously, but there's a limit to how much bad news a person can take. I'm sorry," she said a split-second later. "I didn't mean it that way." Darby, Pratt, she didn't need to educate Jordan on how it felt when the hits just kept coming. "I'm sorry," Ellie said again, too many times today. "I'm tired, and I'm not at my best this morning. I'll file a report first thing when I go in tonight."

"Or you could come with me, and we do it together."

"Please. I really need to sleep."

"You'll have enough time. I'll drive you. I need to check something. That bastard is not supposed to send messages from prison, so there must be someone who provided him with the phone."

Even in her exhausted state, it came through to Ellie loudly and clearly what Jordan had said. "No, I don't think so. There's no way he can get to a phone, and besides, why would he...no. That doesn't make sense."

"You were the originally intended victim," Jordan reminded her. It was the last thing Ellie wanted to hear after her shift and the emotional conversation with her friends, after her nightmares from that night had faded, if replaced by others.

"Well, thanks for the reminder."

"I need to make sure you're safe," Jordan said, making no attempt to apologize. The strange thing was, Ellie could understand her reasoning, even if she didn't like it. She was trying to keep the big picture in mind, how it wouldn't serve Jordan at all if her colleagues thought she was on a wild goose chase. The mere idea that she could be right, though, opened up a bottomless pit of fear. Neither of them could be completely rational when it came to Darby. They would have to enlist help. With a sinking heart, she realized that it would probably be some time before she got to sleep.

"Please, do that for me. If it's nothing, I'm sorry, and I'll owe you for keeping you awake, but I can't stand..."

Jordan's fears were on a different scale after those days in Darby's basement. There was no way Ellie could tell her no.

"Let's go find out," she said.

Chapter Twelve

E llie was silent during the drive to the station, probably more from fatigue than irritation, Jordan reasoned. It wasn't irrational to make sure the anonymous sender wouldn't go from a nuisance to a real threat—it might be a tad irrational to assume Jonathan Darby cared enough to orchestrate this scheme, but she wasn't willing to take any chances.

If she had to scare Ellie in order for her to take this seriously, Jordan wasn't above that, even if she was sorry.

She knew Darby and his work. It was a mistake to hesitate or show weakness with him. If there was a guard who allowed him to send these messages to Ellie, it had to stop, for both their sake. Jordan was well aware that she might look a bit frantic to Ellie. She couldn't help it. After filing a report and having the number traced, her hectic activities came to an abrupt halt when she saw Detective Doss sitting at her desk with someone familiar: Kathryn Larson.

"Could you please wait in the break room? I'll drive you home in a few," she said to Ellie who nodded, resigned to her altered schedule. Jordan followed her inside, and they shared a quick kiss before the door opened and a uniformed officer walked inside in search of caffeine and sugar.

"I won't be long," Jordan promised.

"No problem."

Just as well that Ellie was more tired than freaked out. Maybe they'd be lucky, and it was nothing but a stupid prank.

You already know it's never that easy, don't you?

"Detective, can I talk to you for a moment?" she addressed Doss, aware of Kathryn's curious look. Whether she knew or not, it didn't matter. She had no place in Jordan's life any longer.

"Sure," Detective Doss said, looking surprised. "I'll be back with you in a moment, Mrs. Larson."

"What is she doing here?" Jordan asked as soon as they were out in the hallway. She didn't like the uneasy expression on Doss's face.

"I thought you weren't on the case anymore."

"I still work here."

"Okay, sure," the younger woman said nervously. "She came in because she had information on Hobbs."

"What? Just like that? Why do you think you can believe her?"

"Because right now, he's in an interrogation room with Henderson. No trace of Pratt yet, but we assume it's only a matter of time."

Jordan leaned back against the wall, trying to come to term with this image, Kathryn having a hand in Hobbs' arrest. Through the glass of the double doors, she cast a glance at the woman, wondering if she should feel something, or what would be appropriate to feel in the first place.

She couldn't wrap her mind around the idea that Kathryn could have done something to benefit someone other than herself. She and Jim weren't that kind of people, not in her experience.

"Is that all?" Doss asked. "I was just going to finish up with her."

"Yeah, sure, go ahead."

She hadn't forgotten about her promise to Ellie, but Ellie understood the priorities in police work. She could probably hold out a moment longer until Jordan had figured out how the man who slipped through their fingers so many times had finally been apprehended.

She stepped into the observation area, joining the lieutenant and Sergeant Bristol. After what happened at the safe house, this case was even more high profile than before. Hobbs' arrest was good news. She shouldn't feel any regrets that it wouldn't be on her record, not this time.

Everything must have happened very fast. Jordan was certain Derek would have called her if he could have spared a second to do so.

"No trace yet of Pratt?" she asked.

The lieutenant shook his head. "Guess what, Hobbs denies having been near the safe house or TJ Pratt since his escape, says he wants nothing to do with what happened there."

"That's rich. He already killed a man during his escape. What's his angle?"

At this point, her question seemed merely rhetorical. There was no way she could leave now, but hopefully she could find someone who could drive Ellie home. She excused herself and made her way back through the main room where Doss's desk was now empty, and into the break room.

Ellie was fast asleep, her head resting on her arms on the table. She looked almost comfortable.

❧

After making sure Ellie would get home and to bed safely, Jordan headed back to her desk, where the blinking light on her phone alerted her to a missed call from the lab. She was about to call back when she saw Doss return with Kathryn. They shook hands and Kathryn went to leave. She could have avoided walking past Jordan's desk, but she didn't, slowing her steps.

Oh no, not today, not this week, not ever. I have nothing to say to you.

"Jordan," her birthmother spoke in a soft voice. That was unfamiliar. In the home she'd known for the first twelve years, there had been a lot of yelling—when the Larsons and their friends weren't stoned out of their wits. Not all of their guests had stopped at pot, and there had been a lot of drinking going on. It had never been safe.

"What do you want?"

"I don't know…" Kathryn wrapped her arms around herself, hesitating.

"Well, if you don't know, I can't help you. I have work to do here."

"I know, and I'm sorry. I don't quite know how to say this."

"Then don't." It came as a surprise to Jordan that she had even gone this far to make the connection. It wasn't a good one either. She had done well without these people in her life, and Jordan preferred for it to stay that way.

"I saw on TV…I saw what happened to you. I'm so sorry."

"I'm not dead. It's all good. Was that all?"

"Yes…no. I was hoping we could meet. There's something we should talk about."

"Like what, your bad taste in men?" Jordan shot back icily. She had no intention of indulging Kathryn. "I don't care. Look, I heard you helped capture Hobbs. Thank you for that. I need you to go now."

"Can we meet for a coffee sometime? I would like to explain."

"I'm busy." *I'll be forever busy when it comes to that.*

"Okay." Kathryn's shoulders slumped slightly. She was good, Jordan had to give her that, almost believable. "Take good care of yourself."

"Sure. I'm pretty good at doing it myself."

Kathryn nodded, the tight set of her lips indicating that the jibe hadn't gone unnoticed with her. Then she left. Jordan leaned back into her chair, resisting the lure of unwanted memories. How twisted of this woman to use Jordan's worst nightmare for her own redemption.

Then again, Jordan had expected nothing less of her. She couldn't afford to dwell on yet another confirmation of how lucky she'd been to get out of that place.

Jordan picked up the phone and called Forensics, hopeful they might already be able to tell her something about the sender of the anonymous texts. Instead, ballistics from the Mara Lyman scene had come in, and the findings made her jump up from her seat.

Mara Lyman had been killed with the same gun as Jensen Baker, which meant there was a connection between Pratt and the mysterious Carl. Bud. She needed to see her CI again, see if Darla had found out anything.

Maybe they'd been able to hit two birds with one stone this time.

Jordan winced at the violent image, then went to find her boss.

Hobbs' interrogation was still going on. Apparently, there were bits and pieces missing, about the timeline, about how much he was willing to share. He wanted a deal. He wasn't going to get one until he gave them something substantial, but Hobbs still insisted he hadn't seen Pratt outside of the prison.

Outside. That was the key word.

Jordan related the findings to Sergeant Bristol who was still in the interrogation room. Of course, the sergeant was extremely interested in the connection between the drug case and the men who had killed one of his officers, and he agreed with her strategy too. She knocked on the door and asked Henderson to step outside for a moment. He did, looking guilty.

"Hey. I know you would have wanted to see this, but there was no time to call. Larson came in, told us Hobbs wanted to turn himself in—it was all very fast from there."

"I know. That's fine. Let me have a shot at him?"

"Sure, go ahead. We've been hitting walls in there for a while."

"Well, yeah, you know I'm good at banging my head against walls," she said matter-of-factly and went inside.

Hobbs looked up at her with an impassive impression. Jordan was still reeling at the connection between Kathryn and this man, Kathryn and Pratt, bad choice in men indeed. She wasn't a child anymore, hiding in the corner of the bedroom. She put men like this behind bars now. The thought was fairly consoling, even if the trace of unease remained.

"I saw what happened to you. I'm so sorry."

"My colleagues told me what you said—that you were never at the safe house, and you didn't come back to kill Pratt."

"That's the truth. After I got out, I went back one time, to see if he could help me out with money or something. He wasn't there, so I left. I never wanted to kill anyone."

"One of the guards died though."

"I didn't mean for that to happen! It was supposed to be quick and easy."

"I believe you," she said, seeing his eyes widen. "There are a few things though that don't make sense yet, and we hope you can help us clear them up. After all, you do want that deal, and I can tell you we need something good in return for those men you shot during your escape."

"But I didn't shoot them!"

That was something a lot harder to believe. Jordan was willing to humor him for the prospect of results. "You escaped from prison. Who shot the guards if it wasn't you?"

"Bud Ryder's guy. I didn't want to kill anyone, but he said it didn't work that way."

"Bud Ryder, is that another of your prison acquaintances? He helped you with the escape?"

"Oh, no, he doesn't have a record. That guy never gets caught. He came here to do some business and look for his girlfriend."

"Mara," Jordan said, feeling a bit sick as she could guess what was about to follow—not the details, but she was forming a general idea. Someone had dangled Mara in front of Ryder like a prize. "You knew where she was, that she'd been trying to get away from him?"

Hobbs shook his head. "I didn't hear about her until later. Man, I needed to get out of this place. I would have done anything..."

"So you did. Pratt didn't contact you once you were out, but he knew, right? He offered you a way out...You just didn't know what the prize would be."

"No one was supposed to die! I realized when I saw the headlines that he was going to pin the safe house on me, and the guards too. They wanted a distraction from the drug business, I assume. They wanted to hit it big, put the locals out of business. Ryder would get his girlfriend back, and he and Pratt would be at the top of the food chain."

"That's why you turned yourself in," Jordan concluded. "You knew Pratt and Ryder would eventually want to take care of the loose ends."

"Kathryn said it would be for the best. After all, she knows TJ well."

Those words made her stomach churn, but the pieces were finally coming together. If they got to Bud Ryder, they'd get to Pratt as well, and this nightmare would finally be over. She could forget about Kathryn and everything she said. None of it mattered anyway—Jack and Pauline were the only real parents she knew.

"Well, she gave you the right advice. Where do we find this Bud Ryder?"

"You don't find him in just one place. He moves around...and he found connections here pretty quick. If you're lucky, someone else gets to him first," Hobbs shared his assessment.

Jordan wasn't too pleased with it. If someone else got to him, Pratt would still be out there.

⁂

"Suddenly all of this becomes a lot clearer. Pratt is the mastermind behind Hobbs' escape, and he rats Mara, who's probably been hiding for years, out to Ryder," Derek mused as they were heading out for a quick lunch. "All of this while sitting in his little trailer, hiding in plain sight among his friends of low-level dealers and such—even under the full radar of the police."

"Yeah. Doesn't look too good for us, does it?"

Jordan still hadn't decided if she could stomach the idea of food, given her association by blood to a brutal criminal and murderer. The trick was to hide in denial for a bit longer. The problems she was dealing with were bigger than that anyway—the texts to Ellie's phone had been sent from an untraceable account. On the plus side, if Darby was trying to play games with them, it meant that Ellie wasn't in immediate danger, from him, anyway. She shuddered, thinking of the scene at the safe house. It had made a mockery of the term. Derek misinterpreted her reaction.

"I'm sorry," he said quickly. "I didn't mean to imply that your parents were..."

"By all means, imply. They've been dealing and using on and off as early as I can remember, Jim and Kathryn that is. There's

116

hardly anything you can throw at them that isn't true. It's a blessing they figured out how to use contraception at least." Derek didn't say anything to that, but the joke came back to bite her anyway—Kathryn had slept with TJ. The one time she hadn't been careful.

"I understand you're angry, but you know that everyone's aware you have no connection whatsoever to him. You're a good cop. You risked your life to save those women—that's what everyone remembers."

"Flattery before noon?" She laughed, a bit self-conscious about Derek's unusual display of emotion. "You know what? I'll take it."

"You should."

It was on the tip of her tongue to tell him about her plan, but Jordan knew he would try to deter her. She wasn't even sure if it was a good plan, probably not. However, it might be her best chance to ban Darby from her mind, see him for the small, and small-minded, man that he was, not the monster of her nightmares.

Jordan was well aware of the result of memories and trauma, as opposed to the sad reality—Darby's attitudes towards women weren't so foreign, he just gained more attention because he took them to an extreme. Still, the media wouldn't make the connection. Darby, Ryder, Pratt, and many more—their actions might not be common, but what was in their heads, sadly, was.

Darby had punished women for what he considered a deviant sex life. Ryder had punished Mara for leaving him.

"I saw you talk to Roberts at the funeral," Derek ventured.

"Okay, not a good subject. Also, none of your business."

"Just checking. She keeps showing up in unexpected places. First, Marcus's party, and then the funeral. I still think she should have faced one hell of a lot more disciplinary action for what she did."

His anger surprised her.

"I'm not keen on defending her under the best of circumstances, but her plan worked after all. She drew Darby out. Look...He kept tabs on the investigation like every good little serial killer does. He'd already attacked one of ours, so you can't tell me that it's only because of Bethany he got interested in me. That just gave him the specifics."

Derek's expression was grim, and she didn't need to ask further clarification. The video. Her stumbling apology to Bethany, according to the misogynist madman's script. When she thought about it now, the instant reaction was shame, though at the time she had been too distracted by pain and drugs to feel it.

"It's not like I was never going to see her again. She's friends with Jensen Baker's family. I'm all right. I need you to stop second guessing that. Instead, let's discuss some ideas on how to find a ghost, because apparently, very few people have even seen him. I want to take another look at Mara's history, see if we can pinpoint where and when she met him. That might give us an idea about his movements and who he pissed off."

"Always good to know," Derek agreed.

His cell phone rang, and Jordan could tell from his expression changing in the course of the brief conversation that the news wasn't good.

"Apparently, he made some enemies here as well. Remember Tyler Yates? He was just found killed, the same way as Lyman, only a block away from Lyman's apartment building. That's not a coincidence."

"I didn't think so."

At this point, Jordan was grateful for lunch being canceled. She had arrested Yates five years ago. He was out on parole.

Jordan had been vaguely aware. Apparently, he got back into the trade, and in the way of a new dealer in town.

Chapter Thirteen

T he crime scene was almost a replica of Mara Lyman's, the message clear: Ryder was warning the players in town not to mess with him. Jordan noticed Detective Doss's slightly disappointed expression when she realized Derek had not come alone. Jordan couldn't blame her. She preferred working with Derek too.

If Doss had other motives though, she might be the one colleague of theirs who was blessedly unaware of all the rumors that had been surrounding Jordan for a while. She'd never minded them—at least, having a reputation meant that someone cared. Lately, she wasn't so sure anymore. The idea that her family history and theories might be discussed behind closed doors made her sick.

She was probably paranoid. Her friends didn't think of her in terms of her connection to Pratt. She had to believe that.

If that was at all possible, they got even less out of the neighbors than with Mara's murder. People didn't trust the police much, but that wasn't all there was to the story, Jordan reflected after curt interactions, and doors almost slammed in their faces.

Darla called when Jordan was getting ready to update the night shift on the day's findings.

"I'm not sure if it's something, but I ran into an old friend of mine who had something interesting to say."

"That's great. Go ahead." She was thrilled they finally had an angle with Pratt, not so much about the fact that it had taken another death. The sooner they could wrap this up, the better.

"Um...not so fast? You owe me."

"Well, I've got to know what it's worth. You said you're not sure if it's anything."

Darla gave an exaggerated sigh. "Can't you meet me? I could use something sweet. I thought you guys always have donuts around?"

This had been a bit of a running gag between them for a while, but at the moment, her reference made Jordan's stomach growl. Hours had passed since the canceled lunch. "You know what, food is a good idea. Let me wrap up here, and I can meet you in an hour or so, the usual place. I'll see you then—and keep your head down."

Darla laughed. "Always. See you later."

"That's the plan."

Jordan headed downstairs for the roll call, but stopped when she saw Ellie at her desk, talking to Kate McCarthy. She walked over to greet them, hoping she could have a semi-private moment with Ellie and apologize for abandoning her earlier.

"McCarthy," she said. "It's good to see you."

"Thanks. I figured being here would be more helpful than sitting around at home. Libby feels the same. She'll be back next week."

"I'm glad to hear it. Can you excuse us for a moment?"

"Sure."

The smile she gave Ellie didn't go unnoticed by Jordan. As soon as Kate was out of sight, Jordan perched on the edge of Ellie's desk and snatched a piece of her sandwich. "I'm sorry. I had to skip lunch thanks to the Yates case, now I can barely control myself around food anymore."

Ellie couldn't stifle the smile. "I'd say barely is a euphemism since you're already having my dinner."

"I'll make it up to you. As you know, I still have a fridge full of breakfast food."

"Oh. I wasn't sure if you wanted me to—"

"I don't have a lot of time," Jordan said quickly. "I'm sorry for leaving you this morning."

"I understand. I heard there's been a lot going on today."

"Yeah. There's something else though. We couldn't trace the phone from which those texts were sent."

Ellie looked thoughtful. "I guess that's it, then. I haven't had any messages all day. Maybe he's giving up. Whoever that jerk is, he doesn't scare me."

Maybe that's because you're braver than me. "I'm not leaving that to chance," Jordan said.

"What are you going to do?"

"We'll see."

Obviously, that wasn't vague enough for Ellie, who shook her head. "If it involves anything about Darby, let it rest. I'll get a new phone, and that'll be the end of it. He's safely locked away. That's all I need to know."

Yes, but what if it's not enough for me?

"I need to go," Jordan said. "I'm meeting my CI later. She might have something. You'll be out with Kate tonight?"

"Yes. Casey has the night off. Jordan, please, promise me you won't do anything that could cause you problems, not on my behalf. Those were stupid pranks. There are other cases."

"Stop it. It makes me look bad when your approach is the more logical one."

"What's that supposed to mean?"

"Nothing." Jordan used the rare moment of few witnesses around them to reach out and tuck a strand of hair behind Ellie's ear. "I look forward to breakfast."

"Me too," Ellie murmured. "Don't forget what I said."

She wouldn't like it. Derek wouldn't like it, and they probably had a point, but this was for her own peace of mind. Backing down from the idea would make her feel like a coward, and that was the kind of low Jordan never wanted to experience again.

⁓

"I want you to keep eyes and ears open, not only for Pratt, but for Ryder," Jordan told her attentive audience at roll call. "He might go by Carl or Bud, very few people have seen him, but he's already made some friends and enemies. How he's dealing with the latter, well, we saw that with Lyman and Yates. Let's find this guy."

Kate and Ellie sat together at a table. Behind them, another uniformed cop raised his hand. "What about Kathryn Larson? She seemed to know all of these men pretty well." He made quotation marks with his fingers.

For a moment, Jordan was perplexed to find that she couldn't worry about the disrespect towards a woman who owed her so much. This, however, wasn't about Kathryn being a failed parent, but about her being a woman. For a moment, she felt nauseated to think that she would have fit Darby's victim profile to a "t", a woman who didn't bother with the rules of convention. If it had been just this one misstep, Jordan would have been in a bad place to judge her. Jim Larson was far from the idea of an ideal partner.

As it was, Jordan felt quite comfortable judging her, not for cheating on her husband, but for having a child when she had no intention whatsoever to take care of her.

"Yes, but at this point, she's not a person of interest. She came forward to give the police information about Hobbs' whereabouts, and we have him in custody. We don't believe she knows anything else that could be relevant to this case."

The young man nodded, obviously satisfied with her answer. Jordan took a deep breath, avoiding Ellie's gaze. Ellie always did her homework and read up on cases as much as she could—even if it weren't for their relationship, this question would have never come from her.

"Be careful. Ryder is responsible for the shootings during Hobbs' escape, but also the safe house, Mara Lyman and probably Yates. Any sighting of him, you call for backup immediately."

"Thanks, Detective Carpenter," Bristol said to her. "I have nothing to add to that."

One by one, the uniformed cops filed out of the room until she and the sergeant were by themselves.

"We're much closer now," Jordan said to him as they left together. "We get Ryder, and Pratt is going down right with him."

"Can't be soon enough." Bristol's expression was grim, probably thinking of the young officer who had lost his life to Pratt and Ryder's rampage.

"I agree. I'm hoping for some results tonight."

It was some sort of backup plan...If she got a lead on those two men tonight, maybe she wouldn't think less of herself if she bailed on that other idea.

In her car, on the way to meet Darla, Jordan realized it didn't make a difference what anyone thought, of her, or Kathryn. She was the one who had to put the basement behind her, the laughter, the violence, always on the verge of turning into something more horrible. Not only had Darby targeted her for her less than moral ways, but he also had the idea he could somehow turn her, flirting with her even before the mask fell.

Guess what, I read that stupid apology when you held a gun to my head, but I'm with the person I want to be with anyway.

"You let him into your head in order to survive," the department shrink had said. *"Now it's time to kick him out."* Yes, and with him the Larsons, and Pratt.

She should reschedule the dinner with her real parents, Jack and Pauline, sometime soon, bring Ellie to finally meet them. With all the dramatic developments of the past weeks, Jordan couldn't even understand why she'd been so hesitant to reconnect with people who had always stood by her.

If McCarthy could come back from her fiancé being murdered, and Marshall from witnessing the brutal act, Jordan would be able to handle a short conversation with the devil. She'd already been through hell.

Jordan had a soup, black coffee, and blueberry cheesecake—there was no way she could restrain herself any longer in the presence of Darla and her appetite. Fortunately, food wasn't the only thing worth paying for tonight.

"I really needed to see you in person for this, because it's good."

"You told me you weren't sure," Jordan reminded her.

"Can't make it too easy on you, can I? Then again...That guy goes around killing people just like that." She snapped her fingers. "It's pretty scary. I ran into an old friend of mine and found out she got friendly with that guy." Darla shuddered.

"Bud Ryder?"

"If that's his last name, you know more than I do. Anyway. Serena, that's her name, she hangs out with him."

"Which is where?"

"I don't know," Darla said.

Jordan groaned. "All right, what else did she say?"

"Well, she might be able to meet you, but she's scared. Everyone knows about the safe house, so they're thinking if Bud could do this, the promises from the police that you can protect us aren't worth all that much." Darla shrugged. "Just passing it on."

"Can you get her to meet me? This is important, Darla. The body count's already too high."

"Well, yeah, I don't want to be added to it, okay? I need to be careful with her."

"Tell me where I can find her," Jordan insisted. "We'll take care of the rest, and your name never even needs to be mentioned. We can go right now."

Darla shook her head. "No. I can't do that. Tomorrow night maybe."

"Okay. I get it. This can break the case. I promise you I appreciate your contribution." Jordan laid the bills out in front of her, a hundred instead of her usual twenty. "If this pans out, I'll double it. Now where can I find Serena?"

"Nope, it doesn't work that way." Darla got to her feet, even though she hadn't finished her plate of pancakes, and took a twenty. "You have to let me work at my own pace. You of all people should know what's at stake."

Jordan picked up the rest of the money, left enough to pay for their food, cursing just another interrupted meal. "Darla, wait. I know exactly what's at stake," she said as she hurried after a stubborn Darla. "I don't want you to take too high a risk, but I need a break. If you can get it for me, I swear, I can help you more than buying you pastry every once in a while."

Darla turned around, giving her a wry look. "Thank you for that, but in order to enjoy that new life you're talking about, I need to be *alive*. I'll bring you Serena when she's ready."

"Don't make me regret this," Jordan warned.

"Did I ever lie to you?"

Jordan relented, realizing she'd have to accept the delay. One more reprieve, a couple of hours spent with Ellie, and she'd find out how far she'd really come in her efforts to move on. She drove home to the bright light of the full moon, the clear night surprising after all the rain lately.

At home, she called Derek to confer briefly and make sure she was still up to date with the course of events. There was a woman's voice in the background she easily identified as Detective Maria Doss.

Jordan disconnected the call, amused. This was the problem with their profession—it was hard to meet someone outside of it, and the moment you started dating, somebody always found out. She opened the door to her fridge, thinking that one of these days, she should learn to cook. She hadn't completely gotten used to the fact that distance from the city also meant distance from all its comforts. At least she'd stock up on frozen dinners the next time, because she only had a few of those left.

She opened a beer for herself and put a frozen Chicken Tikka Masala into the microwave, reflecting on her day while she waited. A stalling tactic to delay having to deal with tomorrow's appointment. She had to make it quick, control the structure of the conversation, keep a handle on her emotions. He'd be watching for any signs of weakness, looking to exploit them—make no mistake, he'd be thrilled to see her.

This wasn't about giving him the satisfaction—it was all about her, and Ellie, of course. The beep of the microwave made her jump.

One way or another, the horror would end. It had for Lori Gleason and Judy Lawrence who had banded together to raise money for victims of violent crimes.

It would end for Jordan too. Starting tomorrow.

After her late dinner, there was still too much time to fill, so she decided to go for a walk. She had found a home in what Bethany would call a cookie cutter neighborhood. It felt safe and cozy, a much-needed contrast to almost everything else in her life right now. Maybe one day, she'd even get a dog. That was as far as Jordan could plan ahead. In the early days with Bethany, she had sometimes thought about having children, but then their relationship started to deteriorate. Besides, with her own history, it might be kinder to give up the thought altogether.

Jordan wasn't sure she was ready to do that. Lately, she'd been confronted with the meaning of parenting a lot—Jim and Kathryn certainly hadn't set the bar too high. She almost laughed when she imagined bringing the subject up with Ellie sometime soon. No, it was better to wait with that. This thing between them had started out as a last resort, and while they were carefully building a foundation, they still had to see where it was going.

Jordan realized they hadn't spoken about Ellie's plans to take the detective's exam in a while. Maybe that was a good start to gauge the temperature. She had thrived on Ellie's initial hero worship more than she cared to admit.

Jordan was still afraid that Ellie might change her mind, sometime along the way, when she realized that Jordan wasn't so heroic after all.

She pushed that thought aside, focusing on more practical matters. She had to remember to take the garbage out tonight. One of the neighbors far down the street had done some renovations, the smell of paint and something else wafting in the cool night air, and all of a sudden, she stopped in the middle of the sidewalk, desperately clinging to the present. For long, terrifying moments, she couldn't move, trapped and strung up by heavy chains. He might return and kill her at any moment.

He might never come back and leave her here to die.

Jordan was back in the present, feeling slightly disoriented when the neighbor spoke to her.

"Ma'am, are you okay? Mrs. Carpenter it is, right?"

If he knew her name, it was only because of the newspaper, not because Jordan had made time and effort to socialize. To his credit, he seemed more genuinely concerned than curious.

"Detective," she said. "Yes, I'm fine, thank you."

"Have a good night."

"You too." Jordan walked on, spooked by the flashback. They had been more frequent in the beginning, manifesting themselves more in nightmares than daytime incidents. She couldn't afford any of this tomorrow—or ever. Maybe she had skipped the gym a few times too often. There was comfort in habits, or else it wouldn't have taken her this long to say goodbye to Bethany.

Chapter Fourteen

T he morning air was frigid. On her way, Ellie had entertained herself with fantasies of a hot shower she might share with Jordan, and a lovemaking session as quick or slow as Jordan's schedule would allow.

She wasn't going to bring up the texts again. They had stopped, so whoever had sent them obviously lost interest. In any case, she didn't want Jordan to give them too much importance though she could understand that any possible connection to Darby had to raise red flags for her. It did that for Ellie too, but now it was over, no reason to dwell on it any longer. She planned to distract Jordan best she could.

It turned out Jordan didn't have time to be distracted this morning. She had, however, a delicious breakfast ready, almost enough to console Ellie. What did the trick was her work outfit of today, a dark blue suit that was different from her usual wear. Ellie had a hard time keeping herself from staring.

"You got any more texts?" Jordan asked when they sat down to eat.

Oh, for Pete's sake.

"No," Ellie said. "I think they got the message. How did your meeting go?"

"So, so," Jordan said vaguely. "I hope to learn something new today."

Ellie waited, but Jordan didn't explain, and they sat in silence for a few moments. She caught Jordan glancing at the clock on the stove.

"Do you have to be somewhere? I assume it's a court day? I can let myself out, if you want."

"No. No, it's fine, finish your breakfast."

"Okay. Sure." Ellie tried hard not to be too paranoid. After all, Jordan had a lot on her mind. It would be a while until their relationship would become the normal she was hoping for. They were seeing each other on a regular basis outside of work. At the moment, she couldn't ask for more. "Would you like to do something on the weekend? Go out, maybe, or order in?"

"I thought maybe we could reschedule dinner with my parents, Pauline and Jack, I mean. I haven't called them yet, but I'm sure they'd be happy to see us."

"Yes. I'd love that." She was tired, Ellie reasoned, so it was probably just her imagination that Jordan could be pulling away. She and Bethany had been together for a long time—it was okay to be cautious. Given the opportunity, Ellie would prove to her that she was worth taking the chance. "I can't wait until the night shifts are over," she said. "I could cook us something."

For some reason that made Jordan laugh. "I'm luckier than I deserve. Sometimes I can't believe that there's still someone willing to cook for me."

"Well, you've made me breakfast every day this week—and I'm willing to do more than that for you, as you know."

"Yeah. Sadly, not today." Jordan stole another glance at the clock. "I'm sorry, but I need to go. Do you want to go home or stay here to sleep?"

"Since you're asking, I think I'll stay. Have a good day. Can I borrow a shirt?"

Already in the doorway, Jordan paused and came around to kiss Ellie. "Sure you can. You know where to find it," she said.

"See you." She left Ellie with the unsettling feeling that there was a lot she hadn't said.

Ellie tried to fight her rising worry by clearing the table. Nothing was wrong. Jordan would have told her if there was anything she needed to know.

She chose a nightshirt from a drawer, secretly thrilled that Jordan allowed such a rather intimate gesture. Besides, her bed was a lot more comfortable than Ellie's, or maybe that was her imagination too.

Chapter Fifteen

T he dress code at work was pretty lenient, so you could see detectives in everything from suit and tie to less formal attire, depending on personal preferences and assignment. Jordan preferred casual on most days—not that it happened every day, but in case she had to run after somebody, it was more efficient to do it in comfortable wear. What she was planning today was far from comfortable.

In order to be successful, she needed to distinguish herself from the perception Darby had, from the woman he thought he knew so well. Her usual court outfit, a dark blue suit, would do. Fortunately, Ellie hadn't asked too many questions this morning.

Jordan didn't want to overdo it either—she was going into a maximum-security prison after all, and she didn't want to draw any more attention to herself than absolutely necessary. As she stood in front of the gates, she wondered if it there could have been anyone to help prepare her for this, if she should have talked to anyone, Derek, the department psychiatrist...Bethany even.

Jordan guessed that all of them would have told her not to take the bait, to stay far away from Darby, and probably, they would have been right.

She couldn't take the risk though. For her sake, or Ellie's, she wasn't sure if it made any difference anymore.

Jordan had hoped for distraction from the disastrous state of things, with her birthparents, at work where everyone was still reeling from the death of one of their own—this was not the kind of distraction she'd hoped for, but so be it.

Maybe after seeing Darby shackled and in a prison uniform, she could truly carry on with her life.

Since she had checked in with the prison officials the other night, the warden wasn't even surprised to see her. Jordan had visited convicts in a maximum-security ward before, knew the drill, how to behave. None of those earlier experiences prepared her for the moment they brought in Darby, and her stomach lurched as if she was on an elevator that had been falling a few stories. *Stay in the present—at all costs.*

However, Jordan noticed he looked surprised, if pleased, to see her. He was that good.

Under the table, she wrung her hands together. Her shoulder ached. The screeching sound of the chains being wound up sounded in her ears, distantly. She waited, her heartbeat thundering in her ears.

"Now I understand why my cell was searched last night," he said. His tone sounded as if they were two strangers making small talk. He leaned forward.

Jordan forced herself not to shrink back. There was no way he could touch her—not physically, at least.

"Are we already doing this, Jordan? Not that I'm complaining. It's good to see you again. You look stunning."

"Cut the crap. You know exactly why they searched your cell. Well, be prepared for that source of yours to dry up, and you better find another hobby."

He smiled widely. "It's delightful talking to you, even though there are so many other things I would love to do...but honestly, I have no idea what you're talking about."

Time to change tactics. It didn't matter if she was feeling sick—if this had the desired results, it would be worth it.

"I know you've been writing messages to Officer Harding. Tell me who helped you, and maybe we can talk about...perks."

"Perks?" He laughed. "This is fascinating. I didn't send any messages—how would I?—though I very much resent the fact that you're still sleeping with her. Don't you remember any of our lessons? If I had the chance to communicate with anyone on the outside, don't you think it would be you?"

That threw her off for a moment. Jordan shook her head with a wry smile. "No, that would be too obvious."

"Maybe," he admitted. "You know that Dr. Roberts told me a lot about you. I'd grown quite fond of her."

She suppressed the shudder. That either meant he had imagined Bethany half naked and helpless, or he saw her as a capable sparring partner. At the moment, Jordan wasn't sure which was worse. "Do you know she once wondered if you were really a lesbian?"

Wow, Bethany, was her first thought, even though Jordan knew she was dealing with a psychopath for whom the truth was nothing more than an afterthought. She knew Bethany had tried to bait him by telling a story that in fact did overlap with the somber reality between them, but she wouldn't go that far...would she? Jordan had read her report. There was nothing about this particular detail in it. If Bethany had indeed gone there, she'd made it up—it was impossible that in all the years they'd spent together, she wasn't sure. Bethany didn't invest in anything or anyone she thought wasn't worth her time.

"Whatever you're up to, stop. You lost."

There was a gleam in his eyes, something she remembered well. "My own Clarice, trying to solve a mystery..."

"Don't flatter yourself."

"In any case, I'm sorry I can't help you, Jordan. I admit I didn't approve of your immoral behavior, but at least you apologized, remember? I believe the police department kept that video for evidence. I remember that moment fondly, and so should you. Harding...I realized soon that she was beyond redemption, so I didn't have much interest in her."

"Not even when you attacked her? Stop lying."

He leaned back in the chair, flexing his fingers. Down in the basement, that had never been a good sign.

Stay in the present.

"About that, yeah, isn't it funny how quickly we jump to conclusions? I assume that in the dark, one guy with a ski mask looks like the other, doesn't he?" he challenged.

Something about this exchange didn't feel right, then again, was it a surprise that being in the same room with this man put her on edge? "You confessed."

"Well." He cocked his head, regarding her, clearly enjoying the interaction. What had she ever hoped to achieve by coming here? "There's a difference between the truth and hearing what you want to hear, don't you think? This was the easiest solution for everyone, and frankly, I wanted to make it easy on you. It wasn't your fault that we got interrupted. The pieces fit together so well. For me, it doesn't make much of a difference, but you put two and two together and maybe get an idea who's been sending those messages."

Jordan resisted the urge to jump to her feet. That would mean—and would let him know—that she believed him. She wasn't ready to make that concession yet and acknowledge all it implied.

"You didn't answer my question though. Was Bethany right about you?"

Jordan got to her feet, slowly, as to not make it look like she was running from the room.

"Thanks for nothing. You know, it really doesn't surprise me that a self-appointed moral apostle is a homophobe too. Comes with the territory."

"Oh, come on, Jordan, you know that's not true. I'm not calling the existence of lesbians into question, I'm not that much of a backwards-thinking person. I'm just saying...we got close, didn't we?"

She ignored his words and left the room, thinking she might need to have a conversation with Bethany as well—but first of all, she'd have some work to do.

⁂

Calling Ellie was the first order of business.

"All right...I have to confess something."

Ellie sounded guarded. "I'm listening..."

"I didn't go to court today." In the parking lot of a fast-food restaurant, Jordan leaned back in her seat, feeling cramped and claustrophobic in the confined space. She reached over to open the window, breathing a sigh of relief when a gust of air came in.

"Jordan? Are you okay? What happened?"

"I saw Darby," she said.

"Oh no, why did you do that?"

For some reason, Jordan had been worried Ellie might be angry, but instead there was sadness in her voice. "His cell was searched. They will monitor him closely, but there was no cell phone, no indication that anyone helped him."

"Okay, good. I'm sorry you had to go through this, but you didn't need to do this on my behalf..." Ellie, intuitive as always, knew of course that this wasn't about her only. "Thank you for making sure. Are you okay?" she asked again.

"Yeah. I think." Jordan laughed wryly. "I'll live. It was nothing I didn't expect. If anything, it's good to know that fantasies are the only thing he gets to get off on now."

"So it's over?"

"I'm afraid it's not. He now claims he didn't attack you that night."

Again, a thoughtful pause. It wasn't hard to read Ellie's doubts into that. "How do you know he's not lying this time?"

"I don't know," Jordan said truthfully. "I think we should take some precautions. Sure, he's not exactly trustworthy, but he has nothing to gain from this. If anything, I think he would prefer to make me go back, play me—this way, if we have to focus on somebody else, he's not going to see me again anytime soon."

Ellie sighed. "Frankly, I'm not sure what to make of any of this. He confessed. Can't we leave it at that? He's a pathological liar, and good at it."

"I hate to be such a downer, but...just be careful, okay?"

"Of course. I've got to go," Ellie said with regret. "You be careful too."

"Sure. I always am."

Maybe Ellie was right. Darby would jump at any chance to mess with her mind, but the world didn't revolve around Jonathan Darby, much as he'd like, or Kathryn and Jim Larson. No message from Darla yet. They needed a breakthrough, and after that, it might be time to take some time and take a good look at her priorities.

During the slow disintegration of her relationship with Bethany, Jordan had clung to the one thing she was sure of. She could do this job, and she was good at it, something to weigh in against the bad karma she seemed to be amassing. Then she met Ellie.

Darby took an interest in her, and apparently, TJ Pratt, the wolf in the sheep's clothes, a cold-hearted killer, was her father—just when she thought it couldn't get worse. If she decided to take a break, Jordan wasn't sure what this would look like—from the moment of her rescue, her first and only goal had been to get back to work, now doubts were creeping in steadily.

When they first met, Bethany's boss had handpicked members of a task force, including Jordan. Now she considered getting her paperwork done a major achievement. Something was wrong with this picture.

My own Clarice.

This wasn't fiction. She was terrified and didn't know what to do. It had been bad when she was twelve years old, but it was much worse being an adult and feeling that helpless once more.

Chapter Sixteen

I t wasn't the first bar brawl she'd been called to, but this one, Ellie would remember for some time to come. She had a split-second to prepare herself for impending doom before the elbow connected solidly with her face and a moment later, warm blood spurted from her nose.

The culprit, a man in his mid-twenties, spun around with a shocked expression.

"Oh my God, I'm so sorry, I didn't mean…wait, I'll get you a towel."

"No, you are coming with me," Kate objected before she put the cuffs on him. "Hate to break it to you, but your party is officially over. You okay, Ellie?"

Ellie gratefully took the paper towel the bartender handed her, trying not to make more of a mess than necessary. "I'll live," she said. "Get him out of here."

The host of a birthday party had found out his best friend had slept with his girlfriend—he was going to propose tonight—and things went downhill from there quickly. The owner of the bar had called 911, and here they were, trying to sort out the chaos. Ellie believed the man when he said he hadn't meant to hit her, but that didn't make her any less pissed. At least nothing seemed to be broken.

"There you go." Kate appeared again, out of nowhere, with an icepack. "Now, this was something else."

"Yeah." Ellie sighed. She looked around the broken glass and furniture. "At least we don't have to clean this up. One hell of a party." As she glanced back to Kate, she was surprised to see her friend cracking up with laughter.

"I'm so sorry, I know this isn't funny, but—"

"I get it. It's a little funny when you're not on the other end of it."

Kate still couldn't help herself, holding her belly, tears glistening in her eyes. "It's silly. Really, Ellie, I'm sorry. I haven't laughed like this—or at all—since..."

"I know." Ellie laid an arm around her shoulders. Now that the fight was broken up and everyone involved was waiting for the ride downtown, they could leave as well. Kate wiped her eyes, her expression perplexed as if she still couldn't grasp her reaction.

"It feels good," she said wistfully. "I wasn't sure if I ever could—or should feel that again."

"You'll be okay. It takes time." *Even though you'll never be the same again.* Between the two of them, they knew that those words, spoken and implied, weren't just platitudes. She was anxious about meeting Jordan later. Ellie still felt uneasy about the fact that she'd gone to see Darby on her own. Not all coping strategies were helpful, and she had the impression it might be a little early for this confrontation. There hadn't been any more texts. It wouldn't have been necessary.

She wanted to believe that Darby wasn't behind the texts. However, when it came to the attack, Ellie couldn't wrap her mind around the idea that the perpetrator was still out there. It wasn't possible.

"I meant to ask you something," Kate said when they were back in the car. "Libby will come back to work on Monday. I was wondering if you'd like to hang out after our shift, just a couple of drinks…" She shook her head. "I already feel guilty just saying that. It's not like we have a lot to celebrate at the moment, but I need to do something other than stare at the walls."

"I understand. Sure, Monday night is fine. I'm glad Libby is coming back."

Lately, Ellie had spent most of her free time, if not sleeping, with Jordan. She was happy with that, but she also knew Jordan felt crowded easily. Ellie wanted to be there for her without becoming too overbearing like, for example, Bethany.

She wasn't going to make the same mistakes.

She wasn't the other woman any longer. Ellie knew she had to do better, and she might as well start by giving Jordan some space.

Chapter
Seventeen

Jordan decided it was time to leave—her desk hadn't been this tidy in a long time, and there was nothing much left for her. No message from Darla. Rationally, she knew no one was questioning or rejecting her, yet she felt off, not belonging. The feeling was familiar, if not in her work environment.

She was about to drive home but decided otherwise and took the street to the city center. On the way, she passed the All Colors, a bar where Darby had stalked his victims. His agency. There was a *For Rent* sign in the window.

She might as well squeeze all unpleasant necessities into one day. Jordan had read the reports, knew what Bethany had been trying to do, and she didn't blame her, even though the plan had spiraled out of control. Darby's MO was to punish women he thought to have questionable morals—as in cheating, and he'd offered his services to angered partners of the not so much better half gone astray. Jordan, in his mind, could use some behavior adjustment as well.

When she stepped out of the elevator, Jordan already questioned the wisdom of her current actions. Bethany might not even be home. She should have called.

Yeah, right.

She should have never come here in the first place, after running from their last interaction at the funeral. This wouldn't achieve anything other than giving Bethany the wrong idea. Jordan rang the doorbell, and a moment later, she heard footsteps from within the apartment—nowhere to run now.

"Jordan. Come on in."

Bethany stepped aside to let her in, looking not at all surprised. She was extremely smart and intuitive, and in the beginning, it was something that had attracted Jordan. It was like a game between them, a battle of wits—it became less fun when Bethany always needed to win.

"I won't stay long," she said. "I just need to ask you something." Did she, really?

"Anything." Conveniently, Bethany also seemed to have forgotten about the terse conversation at the cemetery. "I thought you might stop by. Take a seat. You have that long, don't you?"

"What did you tell him?" Jordan preferred to stand in case she needed to get to the door quickly. She noticed Bethany hadn't made any changes to the place. Then again, Jordan didn't have that much input in the first place. "Darby. When you were chatting with him, engaging him, what exactly did you tell him?"

Bethany was still wearing her poker face. "You read the reports. It's all in there. I told him my girlfriend was cheating on me, and he said he'd take care of it. Where is this coming from?"

"I went to see him this morning."

"Oh, honey, that wasn't a good idea. Why didn't you come to me first?"

If Bethany and Ellie agreed on the subject, did that mean she had screwed up badly? "Did you tell him anything that wasn't in the report? Think about it. Did you ever speak on the phone, or in video chat, anything that's not in the records?"

Bethany perched on the armrest of the couch. She might be trying to remember—or stalling. "I had to make it realistic," she said. "There was quite enough material to work with."

"Jesus, Bethany. I hope you know what you were doing."

"It's over. He will never get out."

"You told him I had doubts about..." That was too ridiculous even to say it out loud.

"Well...you had doubts about many things at that point, and you were talking about them when you had a drink or two too many," Bethany said. "I was convinced it would help catch him. I'm sorry." She got up and made a step towards Jordan who stepped back and half turned around.

"I can't believe this. Why?"

"I never meant for you to get hurt. I swear." Bethany came up behind her, speaking softly, but she didn't touch Jordan. "It wasn't worth it. I wish I could turn back time and do it all differently, but it's too late now. I am so sorry. I heard. Officially, it's none of my business. That son of a bitch Pratt is..." Bethany paused.

"My father, yes."

Jordan pressed a hand against her mouth, knowing that she was in the worst possible place to have this meltdown now. Not that it was a surprise—in the wake of the horror, her body and mind continued to let her down. Bethany finally moved in, embracing her from behind. "Baby. I'm so sorry."

"Don't. I need to go."

"Why did you come here in the first place?" Bethany's question was all curiosity, no scorn. Any reason Jordan might have had didn't sound so good to her anymore, in her head, or out loud. Her world was crumbling, had been for some time. She had thought she could get away, from the basement, her parents' trailer, all by being a good cop. Wishful thinking. Her instincts had been letting her down too. She took a deep breath. "To hear it from you. I've got everything I wanted, thanks so much."

"Jordan, wait. Don't run away again. Can't we talk about all this like adults?" This was a card Bethany often pulled when she was about to lose an argument. She looked truly upset, though, a rare, real emotional moment, and more than Jordan could handle.

"I am sorry. I shouldn't have come here. You're right. He's a liar. Why did I even bother?"

"No, it's good you came. Please, stay. We can work this all out. I'll take some time off, hell, I'll quit my job if you want me to, and I'll be here for you. Just let me."

"No." Jordan didn't even blame her—if there was anyone to blame, it was her for being naïve enough to come here and expect anything different. She had known.

"I still love you," Bethany claimed, "and whatever it is you're trying to do these days, I know you still have feelings for me too. Nine years, no one puts that aside just like that. Let me help you. Jordan...I'm afraid for you."

"You don't have to be. I'm sorry if you misunderstood. Take care."

Jordan resisted the urge to slam the door behind her, part of her obviously still worried Bethany could think of her as childish. In the elevator, she turned away from the mirror wall, still holding on.

Barely.

She skipped the gym for another day. Drinking wouldn't change anything, Jordan knew that from experience, but it would, if only for a while, stop the roller-coaster, keep the monsters lurking in the shadows of her mind at bay, Darby, and those further away.

Her grades had been mediocre at best before she got to live with the Carpenters, which wasn't a surprise. It was always loud, a strange, sweet smell in the air she didn't know to name until later. She thought she had let all of this behind her, a long time ago, but going back to the trailer park and talking to Pratt for that first time in many years hadn't done her any good. Jim Larson hadn't been the greatest father material either, proven by the fact that he and Kathryn had never even tried to get her back.

Which was most likely for the best.

"Bad day?" the bartender asked after she gave him her order.

"Life," she returned, and he gave her a sympathetic smile as he put the glass in front of her.

"There you go." He lingered, almost making her pay and turn around. She wasn't in the mood for company, at least not his. "You want to talk about it? My boss wouldn't like it if he heard me say this, but sometimes, drinking is not the answer."

"No," Jordan said, pushing the empty glass towards him. "Get me another one? That works fine."

He refilled her glass and left the bottle on the counter, a silent capitulation, or so she thought. It was odd, she reflected, how blurring the image led to an unwelcome clarity sometimes. She shouldn't be drinking, letting her guard down, inviting images that would further chip away at the safety she'd found. Then, now. Jordan wanted them to go away, instead it seemed like she was putting a spotlight on them.

All she wanted was a break from a reality that seemed to become more disturbing with every moment. Seeing Darby again had reminded her, of the choking fear that he might want to accelerate the plan at any moment, the possibility that he might rape or kill her. Her fingers tightened around the glass.

It was over and done. He lied, just like Kathryn and Jim were lying. Someday soon, she would move on with her life, and none of them had a place in it.

"Look, my shift is almost over," the bartender tried again. "I don't really have anywhere to go, so if you want to talk..."

Jordan shook her head. "Nothing to talk about."

"Let me call you a cab at least?"

"How about you do your job and leave me alone?"

What the hell are you doing, TJ? There was something that had alarmed Jim, jolting him out of his drug-induced stupor. That's what it did for him—he retreated and forgot the world around him, whereas Kathryn got affectionate, sometimes with her husband, sometimes with someone else. Whether it was just the two of them, or others were over for parties, Jordan was mostly left to herself, something she learned to appreciate.

She could handle pain—but when Darby had drugged her, the sensations and images rushing through her mind had sent her into a panic, just like that one time when TJ Pratt had come to the trailer and introduced her to whatever it was they were smoking and sniffing at the time. He thought a twelve-year-old panicking was fairly funny. It was the first time she had ever seen Jim and Kathryn concerned, and it could have been almost worth it if they'd been concerned for her.

Bethany didn't need to be afraid. Jordan had come to terms with the fact that they had never cared, no matter how she felt about the situation. These days, she wasn't depressed about the truth, just angry that they managed to mess with her life once more, Jim, Kathryn, Pratt. This anger wasn't masquerading as anything else. She wouldn't think about taking it out on herself.

"No," the bartender said.

"What the hell? You're afraid I can't pay? Here," she picked up her wallet and threw a few bills on the counter. "Now give me my drink."

"I'm sorry. I think you've had enough."

He probably had a point. One more, or two, and she might pass out, but in comparison, this might be the better outcome.

"Just one more. You can call that cab after."

"Why don't you let me take care of that?" The sound of a voice behind her made her want to black out even more. "Jesus."

If Ellie was the number one person on her list she was too ashamed to face right now, Derek Henderson was a close second. "Go away. I'm fine."

"Let's just get you home, okay?" he said. "Hey, look on the bright side. I'll do it for free."

Jordan failed to see the humor in the situation. "You are not the boss of me. Thank God for that."

"Fine, if you absolutely want to be black out drunk tonight, we'll stop at the liquor store, but we'll do it safely. Now, let's get out of here."

"You're...unbelievable. Damn." Getting to her feet, she immediately held on to the counter as the room started to spin. Derek waited patiently.

"I know it's been a shitty day. You could have warned me before you went for a private conversation with Mr. Darby."

"That would have accomplished—what exactly?" Walking worked all right. Jordan wasn't so sure about a moving vehicle, but she'd have to keep it together. Derek was quite fond of his 1973 Pontiac GTO. "I had to do this. I was sure he was behind those text messages."

"There is no proof."

"Which is worse because that means someone else attacked her that night. It never ends. They never give up. I should have known."

"What do you mean?"

"Nothing. I mean nothing. We need to find him." She hated the small pleading tone to her voice. It reminded her of when Darby had recorded the video—an apology for Bethany, because it was all her fault. Then.

Now.

What the hell was wrong with her?

"God, this is embarrassing. Never remind me of this moment, okay?" This had already gone much too far. Derek Henderson was a good friend, but until a few days ago, he had no idea about the way she'd grown up, or that the friendly couple who had provided him with a few dinners after shifts were not her biological parents. She'd been stripped naked for all the world to see, by Darby, by the recent revelations.

"We all want them behind bars. I understand."

"No, you don't. I don't know what to believe anymore. I'm...I'm scared."

"We'll figure this out," Derek said, laying a hand on her shoulder. It didn't seem patronizing, neither did he appear fazed by her breaking character, but at this point, that wasn't a solace to Jordan. She had no idea what could be.

Chapter Eighteen

After the unpleasant course of events, Ellie had been able to leave her shift early. Sure, she wanted to give Jordan space, but she figured that could wait. It was the first time Ellie used the key Jordan had given her. Sure enough, she arrived to a dark empty house, feeling more like an intruder than a welcome guest.

She sat on the couch, trying to ward off the uneasy feeling. At this time in the morning, where could Jordan be? Restless, she got up and walked into the kitchen. Maybe she should start breakfast for a change? Jordan seemed to have no problems with Ellie making herself at home, but maybe this was crossing an invisible line. She heard sounds on the front porch, something shattering. Ellie carefully opened the door and found herself face to face with Detective Henderson, his gun drawn, pointing at her.

"Relax! I'm allowed here."

"That's right." Jordan giggled, which presented a striking contrast to her overall miserable appearance. "Don't shoot her. Otherwise I'll never get laid again."

Now the pieces of the puzzle made sense, kind of. Ellie didn't blame Jordan for wanting to get drunk after seeing Darby, but maybe her partner could have talked her out of both instead of enabling dysfunctional ways of dealing with a horrible experience. She cast an irritated glance towards Henderson. Had that really been necessary?

"Don't look at me," he said, holding up his hands. "I found her that way. What happened to you, Harding?"

"Bar fight. No, we didn't start it," Ellie said dryly. "Come on in."

"No thanks. I'll head home now. See you guys later—I think. Put some ice on that."

"Yeah, thanks for the advice, and...thank you." She turned to look after Jordan who headed straight for the bedroom. Ellie winced. "She'll regret that tomorrow. Who called you?"

Henderson hesitated only briefly, before he said, "Dr. Roberts said she stopped by...It's not like that," he added quickly. "Jordan ran out on her, and she was worried. You know she went to see Darby?"

"Yes." Ellie told herself that she'd be irrational and petty thinking that it was anything other than that visit into her own personal hell that had made Jordan want to drown her misery in vodka. "Thank you," she said again. "I'll make sure she's okay."

She waited until he had left and turned for the bedroom, not sure what to expect, or what was expected from her at this moment. She'd promised. She'd do her best.

"Hey."

Opening the door, Ellie couldn't help staring when she found Jordan stretched out comfortably on the bed, wearing lingerie. This was kind of unusual. Jordan wasn't big fan, she knew, wearing it herself anyway. "I heard you didn't have such a great day. Well, I can *see* it too, poor baby. Come here. Let me make you feel better."

Ellie stepped closer hesitantly, still assessing the situation. "I'm sure we'll both feel better after a few hours of sleep. Let's just do that, okay?"

She'd had other things on her mind, but not tonight. They'd both need a clear head for the conversations to come.

"Come on, it's all we've been doing in this bed lately, not even at the same time. Ellie…I know you want to."

Ellie laid down next to her, still contemplating what would be the best answer when Jordan leaned over to kiss her, hungrily. For a few moments, Ellie was almost willing to forget that they'd had a terrible time behind them with maybe more to come, that Jordan was drunk and simply trying to get away from it all. She couldn't deny her own body's reaction. Sex might not solve any of their problems, but it had been too long. Still, when Jordan's hand went underneath her skirt, she stopped her—with regret, but nevertheless.

"I meant what I said. I'm here for you, and I won't go anywhere. I just need to understand what happened today."

"I found out a few things." Jordan moved her hand to Ellie's face, brushing her fingers over her cheek. Ellie shivered. There was a reason why she had once abandoned all caution and morals when it came to Jordan, and doing the right thing was hardly the easy one.

"I really tried to do this the right way, listen to what the shrink said, and everyone else. It doesn't matter. Meanwhile, that asshole is behind bars, but he's still here! It's got to stop. I need to move on."

"Why did you see Bethany?" Ellie tried hard to keep her tone neutral, curious, non-judgmental.

"I hoped she might want to apologize. She didn't." Jordan laughed bitterly. "Everything is a Goddamn race with her. I nearly died, but I'm still the bad person here. Bad blood, huh? I'm surprised she didn't say that. See, I've had the odds stacked against me for a long time. Maybe you should get out of here right now. Who wants to deal with this shit anyway?"

Her mood had taken a sharp turn. Jordan pulled the covers around her as if cold all of a sudden.

"Let's talk about this tomorrow—and whatever she said, it's not right. You made a mistake, yes, but unlike hers, it never put anyone's life in danger. As for Pratt—it doesn't matter to me or anyone. We know you."

"You don't!"

"What does that mean?" Ellie asked softly. "Don't you think that I have an idea by now? I'm still here. In fact, I let myself into your house in the middle of the night. That has to mean something."

"That means you're brave. Just look at me." Irritated, Jordan got up to take a shirt out of her dresser, pulling it over her head.

"I'm looking." In fact, it was crystal clear to Ellie what she was in for. Bethany would be around, and it would take her a while longer to accept the facts for what they were. Meanwhile, Jordan would seek her counsel for professional reasons, and she would talk to her period, something she didn't need Ellie's permission for. "I wish you had told me yesterday. I know this wasn't easy for you. Come back here?"

Jordan sat on the side of the bed, her back to Ellie. "I wanted to hear from Bethany that she was sorry," she said bitterly. "Meanwhile, I was feeling so sorry for myself I went out to drink, and that man could still be out there! I don't know what's happening to me. It's like I've lost direction completely."

"That's not true. I mean, it's true that you're feeling that way, but you'll be okay. We'll be okay." Ellie embraced her from behind. "There is no second man. Darby saw a chance to plant doubts in your mind, and he went with it. He knows you care about me. That was all it took." She hoped her words made sense to Jordan, though she wasn't entirely sure. She was tired, and having gotten hit in the face didn't help. Finally, Jordan turned to her.

"You deserve..."

"No." Ellie laid a finger on her lips. "I deserve to have this amazing woman in my life, someone who's brave and kind, not to mention gorgeous and sexy. That's what I deserve, and I got her."

Jordan couldn't suppress the smile at her passionate speech. "I hope you did get your head checked out earlier," she said, but her voice was shaky.

"My head is fine. Come on. Let's get some sleep. If you're a little late today, I'm sure Derek will cover for you. We will take the time to talk, just not right now. Okay?"

To her relief, Jordan nodded, and they lay back down under the covers, soon falling asleep in each others' arms. There was something hopeful in that.

Ellie woke to the sound of a phone, momentarily disoriented and wondering why her face felt this tender, then she remembered.

"Jordan. It's yours."

"Oh God, shoot me now," Jordan muttered and winced. "I'm so sorry. I vaguely remember this is not the first inappropriate metaphor I've used. Sorry. Ouch."

"Yeah, I imagine. At least you did that to yourself."

Jordan answered the call, her attention immediately with the person on the other side of the line. "I understand. No, this is not a bad moment. I'll be right there."

"Are you sure?" Ellie asked when Jordan began to gather her clothes hastily. "You shouldn't be driving."

"I'm okay. This can't wait."

"Let me come with you, then." Ellie quickly threw on some clothes as well. "I'll drive you, and then we can come back here before you go to work."

Jordan looked indecisive, but she nodded.

"Okay, but when we get there, I want you to stay in the car. You do exactly what I say."

It was a relief to see Jordan being back to the woman Ellie knew her to be, focused, and taking charge. In fact, it was a bit of a turn-on too. There was no denying they'd have to talk about last night, but either way, they'd be okay in the end, even if they needed to postpone that conversation for a bit.

Chapter
Nineteen

Only minutes had passed when they arrived at the park Darla had named, the place deserted in the early morning save for a couple of joggers and an elderly man walking his dog. It didn't take Jordan long to establish that Darla was nowhere to be seen. She went back to the car to call her.

Darla had turned off her phone.

"Damn it," she cursed before sitting back in the passenger's seat.

Ellie cast her a curious glance. "I know I'm not supposed to leave the car, but can I ask?"

Of course, Ellie had so many questions, mostly because Jordan had been dodging many of them as long as she could. This wasn't one of the subjects she was trying to avoid.

"My informant? She said she could put me in touch with someone who knows Ryder. She said it was urgent...but here we are."

"Do you think something might have happened to her?" Ellie asked, swiftly uncovering Jordan's worries.

"I don't know. I will try to find her. There are places where she usually hangs out. I can ask around, but I want to go back to the station, put the word out. This isn't good." She picked up her phone again. Fortunately, Derek picked up on the first ring. Jordan had a faint memory of last night's interactions that made her cringe.

"I told the boss you were sick, probably calling in later today...I hope," he said, keeping his tone light, but it wasn't hard to read between the lines.

"Thanks, you're the best. That's not why I'm calling. Darla Pierson—she was supposed to meet me this morning, regarding Ryder, didn't show up. I have some ideas where to look, but I'll need some help. I want to make sure she's not in trouble."

"I'm on it," he promised. "You better make that call?"

"I'm coming in," she said. "Don't worry, I'll clear things up with the lieutenant."

"That's what I'm counting on, Carpenter. I want to see you in my office ASAP," the man in question said from the other end of the line.

Even Ellie flinched a bit at his tone. "Ouch," she said after Jordan had disconnected the call.

"Yeah. Ouch. Would you mind being my designated driver for a little while longer?"

Jordan reached over to take Ellie's hand. "I swear, sometime soon I'll be the responsible adult I used to be at some point, before all this shit started, and we'll talk."

"Don't worry," Ellie said. "I told you, I won't go anywhere. Do you still want to stop by your house?"

Jordan took a look at her rumpled clothes. There wasn't much of an alternative. "Absolutely. The 'I just fell out of bed' style might be okay with Darla, but the boss won't be amused if I show up to work like that."

Ellie's sympathetic look reflected what she already knew—she was in for some stern words from her supervisor.

Back at the house, Jordan grimaced at her reflection in the mirror. The quick hot shower made her feel slightly better, but it hadn't done anything for her complexion or the dark circles under her eyes. Why had she done that to herself?

That's right. Darby. Kathryn. Bethany, who knew how to put her finger in the wound, and did so gladly, because she believed in confronting fears when they weren't her own. Jordan shook her head, then holding on to it with both hands.

Ouch.

So, she'd had lousy birthparents, wasted years on a relationship that hadn't done her or Bethany any good, and crossed paths with a sadistic killer. More importantly, she had come out alive every time, and there were still people in her life willing to bet on her.

Now was not the moment to get emotional either, she reminded herself, wiping a tear from the corner of her eye.

Unfortunately, she had somewhere to be.

****

Ellie had dropped her off at the station and then went home to get her own day started.

"Carpenter," the lieutenant greeted her when Jordan knocked on the door of his office and reluctantly went inside. "I was beginning to wonder whether we would see you today. It's very considerate of you to show up after all. What's this mysterious sickness your partner was talking about, if I may ask?"

"I'm sorry," she mumbled. "I was meeting with a CI this morning, about the Ryder case, and Pratt, but she didn't show up. I know I'm technically not supposed to be on that case, but—"

"Not just technically, but since those two cases so conveniently overlap, it's not why I wanted you here. Sit." He got up to open his door. "Henderson! Do you have a minute?"

The list of people she owed was getting longer. Derek walked inside, appearing much too calm for the conversation to come—or maybe he had expected it all along.

"Lieutenant?"

"I know you guys know your job, there's no question about it. However, in order to do my job, I need to be informed about what's going on every once in a while, don't you agree? Detective Carpenter, what was the reason again for seeing Mr. Darby, not to mention making Henderson cover for you?"

"She didn't actually—"

"I'm not talking to you right now."

"This was about text messages Officer Harding got," Jordan defended herself. "They bordered on threatening, and there was a clear reference to the attack. It made sense to assume Darby could have found a way to send them, via a guard maybe."

"Did you find any evidence that this was the case?"

Jordan bit her lip. "No."

"Did you learn anything of importance from the alleged mastermind himself?"

"No...but...He killed three women, at least. I *needed* to make sure."

Derek cleared his throat discreetly, alerting her to the fact that her voice had risen quite a bit.

"Jonathan Darby denied having attacked Officer Harding," Jordan continued. "I understand that he might be lying, but what if that's not the case? That means the real attacker is still out there!"

"This is exactly why it was a bad idea to go by yourself without clearing this with me first. Your private life is your business, but obviously Darby is aware of your relationship with Harding. He got into your head."

"That's not all..."

"Listen, Darby will spend the rest of his life in a maximum-security facility, for which, believe me, we're all grateful. For now, I need you to concentrate on Ryder and Pratt, not some side investigations that a psychopathic killer suggests you might do. Are we clear?"

"Crystal clear, sir." At least he hadn't suggested she'd take a vacation.

"Henderson, this is not high school. The next time you come to me first."

Derek nodded, unfazed by the criticism. "Will do."

"All right, you two, get back to work—and Carpenter, when this case is closed, you will take some time off."

Jordan breathed a sigh of relief when they were on the other side of the closed door. "Thanks for trying. I owe you. You want to come for dinner with my parents too?"

He laughed. "You don't think it would be awkward? How about you pay for coffee for the next month?"

"Oh, you drive a hard bargain. Speaking of coffee, I could use some. Did you get anything on Darla?"

"No, nothing."

Jordan nodded, feeling queasy at the thought she might have pushed her too hard.

"She knows the risks."

"I'm aware. This is still strange. I'd like to hit the bars tonight, check if anybody's seen her. There are a few places I know she hangs out on a regular basis, especially when she wants to be under the radar."

"Okay. I'll come with you."

The following silence was laden with meaning, not hard to figure out for Jordan.

"I promise, you will never again get a phone call from Bethany in the middle of the night. That was stupid, and childish." Kind of appropriate though, considering she was still dealing with that frightened child of so many years ago.

"It hasn't been that long," Derek said. "You should cut yourself some slack."

Jordan knew he was right, but she wasn't sure if a couple of weeks under palm trees could scrub her mind clean of the nightmares. Getting Pratt behind bars, and his buddy Ryder too, would go a long way towards achieving that.

Chapter Twenty

E llie should have gone home, do some cleaning and grocery shopping, or figure out what to wear for the dinner with Jordan's parents. Somehow, she couldn't make herself leave the house where Jordan was trying so hard to make a home for herself in the aftermath of her trauma.

It was a beautiful place, no doubt about it. Then again, she'd made a deal with the Devil to get it—that's where Ellie's doubts came in. However, she had to trust that Jordan knew what would help her move on. As long as Ellie was included in that vision of the future, she could keep her promise and be patient. She couldn't even imagine what Jordan was going through with the latest revelations.

What Libby had said was true though. They wouldn't give up trying.

She walked around, cup of coffee in hand, wondering if at some point they would make plans to live together. In fact, they practically did, with Ellie arriving after her shift every day and sleeping in Jordan's bed while she was at work. Neither of them had mentioned in so many words what it meant or could mean. Ellie could sympathize. She was hurt when Rhonda had moved out so abruptly, leaving one month's rent behind. For too long now Ellie had been paying for a space bigger than she needed, too busy to even try getting another roommate.

Jordan, however, had spent nine years in a claustrophobic relationship, so it wasn't surprising she hadn't brought up the subject yet.

Space. Ellie sighed. She stood in front of a bookshelf, then she kneeled, drawn to the box that said 'photos'. Her fingers tingled with curiosity, opening the lid an inch. Ellie got up and stepped back, spooked by her almost transgression.

Jordan was a private person, with everyone. Snooping in the home of someone who had trusted her with the keys was generally a bad idea, no matter how intimate she was with that person. Ellie took a deep breath and sat on the couch, her eyes still on the box, as she finished her coffee.

She would ask.

Chances were there were pictures in that box she didn't want to see, of a happier time with Bethany that must have existed at some point in the past. Nine years. Where had they gone so wrong?

Ellie went back to the kitchen and rinsed her cup in the sink before she let herself out. It was a beautiful place. She could imagine living here someday.

Kate was behind the wheel of the squad car when they got the message from dispatch. *Teenagers report a white female, twenties, presumably dead, near the tracks of Hartwood station. An ambulance is on the way.*

Ellie took the call, and Kate made a sharp turn towards the location. While this was hardly an occasion to celebrate, it made her feel hopeful that her friend was getting back to her usual self, the grief not so deeply etched into her features anymore, though, of course, it was far from over.

They'd all honor Jensen by doing their job the best way they could. The train tracks were only a few blocks away. When they got out of the car, the two teenage girls, pale and shocked, were already waiting for them. One of them was crying.

"Over here."

Even in the dark, it was easy to see the bloody bruises marring the women's face, her clothes stained with dirt. Ellie dropped to her knees, feeling for a pulse. Against the odds, she could feel it, faint, against her fingertips.

"That's all right, sweetie, stay with me." The woman was unconscious but breathing. Ellie carefully checked for visible injuries. No sign of ID in the pocket of the woman's red hoodie.

"Damn," Kate said, her next words drowned out by the sirens of the ambulance, its lights together with the squad car's painting the scene in a ghostly light. Two paramedics came rushing towards them, and Ellie let go of the woman's cold hand, stepping aside to let them work. Kate told them what little they knew. "I'll go with her," she said to Ellie. "Let's get Homicide in here."

Ellie had a bad feeling about this—aside from the fact that this young woman had been beaten up and left to die.

She reached Detective Doss at her desk, hoping against the odds that this violent assault wouldn't become a homicide after all, and the woman could be as lucky as she had been. Ellie was aware of the distant impulse to curl up and cry, but instead she went to take care of the distraught teenagers, finishing their statements and getting them a ride home with another officer.

For a moment, she sat in the squad car, praying she could be wrong, and this wasn't directly related to the disappearance of Jordan's informant. In her heart, she knew she wasn't. Jordan would take this hard.

Chapter Twenty-One

J ordan had two more places left, her frustration and concern growing in the unsuccessful search for Darla. A woman named Charis shared that Darla had shown up a couple of days ago, but she hadn't seen her since. Charis knew Serena. She had, however, no idea where Jordan could find her.

"I wish I knew. I would so tell you if you could get me a date with that guy," she said with a wink, nodding to Derek who had taken a phone call a few feet away.

"I'm afraid I can't do that, but thanks anyway."

Jordan went to get her partner who had just finished the call.

"That was Maria," he said, sounding more serious than she would have liked—definitely not the moment to let him know she was on to him about their relationship.

"Just two more places, I swear, then we can call it a night."

"This wasn't a private call," Derek said. "I think we found her." His next words seemed to come from far away, like under water. "Jordan! She's alive—still. Officers thought it was better to be safe than sorry and called in Homicide, but she's hanging in there."

"What happened?"

"Someone beat her up, dumped her. Maria's at the hospital. They don't have any ID yet, but the description fits."

"Okay. I want to go there. Give me a second."

She went back to Charis's table. The woman gave her a hopeful smile. "You changed your mind?"

"This is important. The moment Serena turns up, you call 911 and call me too." She handed her a business card. "Don't tell anyone we asked for her."

"Sure. That sounds serious. Is she in trouble?"

"Not from us, but she might be in danger. Don't forget it. Call 911 right away," Jordan insisted.

"Yeah, I think I can remember that."

"Just do it."

Jordan joined Henderson again, aware of his concerned looks. At this point, they were more than justified, she had to admit. "I'll be okay," she answered his unspoken question. "This means we're getting close. It will be over soon."

He didn't agree nor disagree.

⌘

"Ms. Pierson can't answer any of your questions right now. She's unconscious," the doctor said with more than a hint of impatience. "At this point, I can't tell you when or if she's going to wake up, but we're doing our best."

"I just need to see her for a moment. Please."

Out of the corner of her eye, Jordan could see Kate McCarthy swallow hard. None of them wanted to be here. She had a debt to pay though.

"Two minutes, no more. This woman is fighting for her life."

Two minutes could be short or long, depending on what you filled them with. Jordan stepped into the room, for a moment overcome with dread. She'd seen too many women bru-

172

talized and murdered, almost ended up dead at the hands of a killer—much as she'd tried to deny it, it was taking more of a toll than she cared to admit. This was almost worse than everything else though. She couldn't shake the feeling that she was at least partly responsible for Darla lying in this bed. Jordan knew, Darla had always worked independently. Like Derek had said, she knew the risks, when to lay low.

"We'll find who did this to you," she said as her vision started to blur. "You'll get through this. I promise you." She hadn't forgotten other promises she'd made to Darla.

She couldn't afford to stop and feel sorry for herself. Jordan brushed a finger over Darla's bruised knuckles, wiping her face before she got up. There was a lot of work to do before she could take that vacation.

If her life wasn't crazy enough, she went back outside to find McCarthy in the waiting area—with Ellie and Bethany and a man she didn't know, wearing a dark suit.

"I'm sorry," both of them said almost in unison when she joined the small group, and a tense silence ensued.

"Okay, hit me," Jordan said, though for the life of her, she couldn't understand why Bethany was here. They didn't need a profiler to figure out Pratt or Ryder. "What is the FBI doing here?"

"As I just told your colleagues, Ryder crossed over into federal jurisdiction with the kind of legacy he's trying to build. Special Agent Russo will assist you on the investigation," Bethany declared far too cheerfully, given the somber circumstances that had brought them here. Jordan sought Ellie's glance and received a slight shrug in return.

"What does that mean, Agent? We turn over our files and you take it from there?" Jordan asked. "Fine. Derek will do that. I have someplace to be."

"If this is about Ryder, then I should come with you," Russo said, making it clear this wasn't just an offer.

"Whatever works for you. We were trying to find a witness previously connected to Ryder by Darla Pierson. Serena Jefferson. It's even more important now that we find her before Ryder does. Let's go."

"Detective..." Bethany sounded unusually uncertain.

"Time is of utmost importance here, as you can imagine. McCarthy, Harding, I want you to stay here in case she does wake up. Derek, get a BOLO out on Serena? We can't be sure that Darla didn't tell anyone about her."

There was a way to break everyone. Everyone.

Jordan spun around to walk away from the scene, Special Agent Russo on her heels.

Chapter
Twenty-Two

"That was awkward," Bethany remarked, and Ellie frantically tried to figure out how the two of them had ended up alone. That's right, Kate had gone to get coffee, and Bethany...She didn't seem to be in a hurry to go anywhere, on the contrary. She might have a sadistic streak...or masochistic, Ellie hadn't yet figured out which one it was. On the bright side, Jordan was obviously holding on, and it looked like they might be able to break the case sometime soon.

"It's probably a good thing that we have a moment," the profiler continued.

No, not at all. In fact, it's the opposite of a good thing. Ellie didn't voice her thoughts but braced herself for a verbal blow. After all, Bethany had made it clear before that she didn't see Ellie as a worthy successor.

"It is?" She couldn't stop the sarcasm from seeping into her tone.

"You started studying for the detective's exam, I assume?" Bethany asked, interested. Two law enforcement officers making friendly conversation, no big deal. Except it was. Where was Kate with that damn coffee?

"It looks like you've taken on a lot lately." Bethany shook her head in sympathy. Ellie couldn't imagine it was genuine.

"You think?" *Don't go there. Don't take the bait.*

"We don't have to do this. We're all adults here, right? Jordan has come a long way, but that latest twist in her family history is really unfortunate. I just wanted to make sure you know she came to see me about Darby…Nothing happened."

For two or three heartbeats, Ellie saw herself at the crossroads. She could take the higher road and acknowledge Bethany's antics for what they were, mind games she would refuse to play. On the other hand…

"What is wrong with you? I know nothing happened, and you know why? I trust Jordan. I know she's in love with me. Don't come to me trying to make small talk when all you want to do is mess with me! We're fine. Jordan is fine. I'm sorry if you're not dealing well with this situation, but that's the way it is. Leave her alone."

"Ellie!" She spun around to nearly collide with Kate who was carrying a tray with three coffees, the liquid sloshing inside.

"What? It's true!"

"Maybe this is not the best place…" Kate ventured.

"She started it!"

Bethany scoffed. "I agree, McCarthy. There's a woman in that hospital room that means a lot to Jordan. You want to be a detective, Harding, and her partner in all things, you have a long way to go. Why don't you start by growing up?"

She didn't wait for an answer from a slack-jawed Ellie, but walked away, her body language conveying triumph.

Kate sat in one of the visitors' seats. "Don't get me wrong, my friend," she said, "but it's never boring around you."

"I wish boring was a possibility for once."

"Yeah." Kate sighed. "I hear you."

Minutes turned into hours, and still there was no news on Darla Pierson's condition. At some point, Kate nodded off in her chair. Ellie was much too wired after tonight's events, and that unfortunate conversation. In an ideal world, Jordan would never have to learn about it. The next best thing was if Ellie could tell her before Bethany did. If she wanted Jordan to open up to her, she would have to return the favor.

She hated how Bethany still made her feel inadequate, on the job, in her relationship with Jordan, even though Ellie knew this was all in her head.

She saw the doctor hurrying their way, and nudged Kate awake quickly.

"Officers? Ms. Pierson is awake. She wants to talk to you."

Obviously, he wasn't happy with the idea but respecting his patient's wishes. Kate and Ellie shared an uneasy look. This probably meant they had to take this chance, or it might be too late to learn anything from Darla.

Chapter
Twenty-Three

S pecial Agent Russo had joined her inside the club, but to Jordan's relief, he didn't mind her taking the lead according to the plan she had laid out for him. Charis groaned when Jordan walked towards her table again. "I told you, I haven't seen her or Serena—and you didn't even bring your partner this time."

"Sorry about that, but he's busy. So am I, so I'll make this short. Why don't you get me downstairs?"

For a moment, Jordan thought Charis might stick out her tongue. She was glad it didn't happen. Jordan didn't have the patience for antics like this, at the moment, or ever.

"You're a cop."

"So?"

"I think you know what that means," a voice said behind her. "Please stop harassing my customers."

"Eddie," she greeted the owner. This bar wasn't the kind of dump Pratt or her birthparents would hang out in, but he'd still be wary about her presence. He had also given her the occasional discreet tip. For the most part, they favored a peaceful co-existence. "It's important that I speak to Serena."

"Serena who?"

"Stop bullshitting me. I'm sure you're aware of a guy named Bud Ryder and the trail of bodies he's been leaving behind."

After a moment of terse silence, he said, "Serena isn't here. I hope you find her."

"I've been told otherwise. Come on, we want the same thing here."

"Which is what?" he asked.

"To keep Serena alive. To make sure what happened to Darla won't happen to her?"

"Darla?"

"She's in the hospital. Someone beat her within an inch of her life. We think it's Ryder. You heard about the safe house too? If he and his gang come busting in here, are you prepared for that?" Jordan could tell that he was about to relent. "Let us deal with Serena," she prompted. "We can protect her. You can't."

"You care about Serena?" he asked.

"I don't want anyone else to get killed. Besides, Ryder isn't good for business. I hear many folks around here would like to see him go."

"You're going to arrest her?"

"I want to talk to her, lay out the possibilities. If that's not possible for me, well, maybe you'd like to talk to my friend with the FBI over there. I'm sure he could find something of interest in here, and I don't think you'd want that, right?"

Eddie nodded. "All right. You better not let me down. Come with me."

There was likely some illegal gambling going on in one of the rooms downstairs, but it wasn't why Jordan was here tonight. She waited for Eddie to unlock a door behind the bar and then followed him down two flights of rackety stairs.

"Fire hazard," she muttered.

"Don't get smart with me, Detective."

"Come on, Eddie. That's my line."

He pulled aside a curtain, revealing what was probably originally a storage area, now holding a bed and a chair. Sitting up against the wall, the woman looked up, alarm showing in her eyes when she saw Jordan.

A frightened woman in a drafty basement held too many dangerous connotations, but Serena Jefferson wasn't in here because someone had taken her. She was hiding.

"Hey, Serena. I'm Jordan, a friend of Darla's."

Serena stared back at her bleakly. "Darla uses that word loosely," she said. "It tells me nothing."

"She says you know where we can find Bud Ryder. Unfortunately, he found her already."

"Is she dead?"

Jordan suppressed a shudder at her matter-of-fact tone. "No, she's not dead, but last I checked the doctors weren't certain that she'd make it. Don't you want this guy off the street?"

"If he knows I talked to you, he's going to kill me."

"No, that's not going to happen. You tell me now, and we arrest him. End of story. If we don't stop him, the killing will continue. Please, let's do this for Darla."

Most of all, Jordan needed to get out of this place that seemed to become more cramped every moment. She felt like she couldn't breathe properly.

"Look, Serena, I'm not trying to trick you. We both know Ryder is dangerous, and so are the people he surrounds himself with. Someone has to step up for all of this to end. Upstairs, there's a federal agent. He can get you protection, but we need you to work with us."

She had made so many promises lately, Jordan felt like a bad liar, but to her relief, Serena nodded. "I will show you, but you have to bring me someplace safe first. It's not a place you can stumble over by accident. You can't just go in like that."

"How did you escape?"

"I didn't," Serena said. "I hid with one of Eddie's friends in a trailer park, and she brought me here when one of Bud's watchdogs came sniffing around and she thought it wasn't safe."

Great idea. Of course, she had firsthand experience that there wasn't such a thing as a good hiding space in a trailer. If Jordan could find Serena by deduction and elimination, and using a bit of pressure and money, anyone could. In fact, Ryder probably wouldn't hesitate to use a lot more of both, and come to the same conclusions.

"That friend, what's her name? This is where Ryder is going to look first."

"Katie, Kathy? She used to deal a bit when she was younger, but she's not into that anymore. A nice older lady, actually. She actually said I should go to the police, but I was so scared. Hiding at Eddie's, Bud would get mad for it, but snitching on him." Serena made a throat-slashing gesture. "You're finished."

Kathy. Jordan felt light-headed. *It's a too damn small world.*

A few minutes later, she caught up with the agent and quickly ushered Serena into the backseat of his car.

"You're not coming?" he asked, surprised.

"I have to go check on something. Get Ms. Jefferson to the department, and don't let her out of your sight. I'll be back as soon as I can."

He frowned. "From where?"

"Something came up," Jordan said. "I don't have time to explain."

She called for backup in the car. Following a hunch by herself had not served her the last time, even though it had saved a woman's life. If she was lucky, she could do it again, this time without collateral damage.

Pratt's trailer loomed darkly when she arrived on the premises, and Jordan remembered her reluctance to come back to this place, the memories it would inevitably unleash. She hadn't known half of it.

This would hopefully be the last time in a long time. Never would be fine too. She drove along the rows of vehicles, telling herself that there was no time to be depressed or sentimental. This wasn't about her childhood, the precarious dance on something worse to happen, but her adult job.

If she'd been honest, Jordan had always known that someday, it would involve her birthparents. Unavoidable.

Taking a deep breath, she knocked on the door.

"Mom? It's me. I need to talk to you." If Kathryn was sulking because Jordan had said no to a cup of coffee, calling her mom would certainly get her attention. She and her husband hadn't given a damn for so long, Jordan had almost managed to return the sentiment.

The trailer was silent, though there was a light inside, and a shadow behind the window.

"Mom? I know you're there."

"It's not a good time," Kathryn's voice floated over to her. "What did you come here for anyway? It's not like we wanted to see you!"

It was impossible not to cringe at those words, no matter how clear the distress. Jordan knocked on the door again. "Let me in," she demanded, placing her hand on her gun. "Now."

"Jordan, please. Leave us alone."

Despite the desperate plea, the door sprang open a moment later, revealing Kathryn, her eyes wide in terror, and the man behind her, holding a gun to her head:

TJ Pratt.

What a messed-up family reunion went through Jordan's head as she stepped into the narrow space.

"Drop the gun!" she yelled, knowing immediately that there wouldn't be a lot of time to make a decision. Pratt might have had backup at the safe house, but he had killed without hesitation or remorse. A former lover—or his biological daughter—would not make any difference to him. "Right now. You might not care about her life, but I can guarantee you, I'm faster than you."

Pratt laughed. "I'll take the chance. See, I told you, Kathy, I was going to kill her. Looks like everything's going according to plan. There'll be no witnesses. Sorry, but you've been getting on my nerves for too long."

Jordan let him talk, keeping an eye on his trigger finger as she moved closer, slowly, trying to get a better angle on Pratt who was still using Kathryn as a shield.

"I know this is not about either of us. It's over, TJ. We got Hobbs, and we're going to arrest your buddy Ryder tonight. Serena is talking to the cops right now. Darla is going to make it. You lose."

"Is that what's going to make you forget about what the guy did to you in his basement?"

"You're sick," Kathryn spat, and he yanked her hair back hard enough to make her cry out.

"Maybe, but you know what? No one will care, trailer trash. That's all you and your whore of a daughter will ever be. Dead whores."

Abruptly, he raised the gun and pulled the trigger.

Chapter
Twenty-Four

"Ellie, there's no time right now," Derek Henderson said, about to get into the car with Agent Russo. Maria had already left with Waters. "We have a location on Ryder. I'll talk to you later."

"Wait! Darla Pierson is conscious and talking. Is Jordan with you?"

"No, why?" Ellie Harding hesitated long enough to test his patience. "If you have something to tell me, do it now. Jordan is on the way to see her—Kathryn Larson," he corrected himself quickly, unsure how much Ellie knew beyond the police reports. "Backup is already on the way. You and McCarthy need to stay put."

"That's where Pratt is going."

"Likely," he admitted. "I need to go, Harding. Jordan will be fine." He hoped his promise would hold up, after all Jordan's situation was beyond complicated. "They were only a few minutes away. Don't worry."

"Okay."

"See you."

He didn't blame Ellie for being scared. Both Ryder and Pratt had proven to be completely ruthless, but they'd both go down tonight, no doubt about it.

Bud Ryder spent a few moments observing the two cops standing in the corner next to Darla Pierson's room. He could have just as easily sent one of his men, but he wanted to take care of her himself—that would send a message to anyone who was so much as thinking about snitching on him.

He slipped inside unnoticed thanks to the scrubs he was wearing. He had seen other nurses go in and check on the patient. The trick was to get in and out quickly.

Pierson was asleep, looking far too good for a person who was supposed to be dead. If you wanted something to be done right, you had to do it yourself...

He stepped closer to the bed, pointing the gun with the silencer at the woman's head.

"Bye-bye, Darla," he said when the distinct pressure against the back of his own head told him he was not alone in the room anymore.

"I wouldn't do that if I were you."

In the glass of the window, he could see the cop, a short blonde woman he could probably take out easily.

He swung around, but she ducked, and the next moment, the other one was in the room, a brunette, taller, training her gun on him as well.

"Step away from the bed," she bitched. "You killed my fiancé. I have no problem shooting you right here. My colleague here won't say anything, neither will Darla, right?"

"Go to hell," Pierson spat, and he slowly lowered his gun, cursing himself for letting a couple of rookies get in his way.

The blonde put the cuffs on him, reading him his rights. This couldn't happen.

"It's okay, Kate. We've got him."

The other woman wasn't listening to her. He could tell she was trouble.

"Kate?" the blonde cop tried again. "Don't do this. He's going to pay for everything he has done."

Cop Kate's finger twitched, and Bud Ryder, the owner of a new drug empire, already feared by the longtime players, pissed his pants.

The men in the house were completely surprised by the team storming the premises. Most of them surrendered, a couple tried to run greeted by cops guarding the entrances. Derek and Maria went from room to room, uncovering a staggering amount of drugs and weapons.

The information Serena had given them was good. This house in the woods was definitely Ryder's headquarters—just no Bud Ryder or TJ Pratt. Derek couldn't reach Jordan. He tried Ellie Harding, but the line was busy too.

"He can't be far," Maria said. "One of his minions will give him up. They don't want to go down for the murder of a cop."

"Unless they're more afraid of Ryder than they are of us. Let's hope—"

His phone rang, and seeing the caller ID, Derek picked up immediately. He could hear someone crying in the background. Kate McCarthy, he realized.

"Harding, what's going on over there?"

"Let me guess. You didn't find Ryder." She didn't sound like she was in acute danger, though her words were troubling.

"You're not saying…"

"It's under control," she said quickly. "He tried to go after Darla Pierson, but it's under control now. We got him. No one was injured. Well, except for his ego. I'll tell you later."

Derek felt slightly uncomfortable at the thought of a couple of rookies dealing with Ryder all by themselves, but they seemed to have done well. "All right. I'll see you at the station."

"Have you heard from Jordan?" she asked. "I can't reach her."

"Not yet. I'll let you know when I know more," he promised. Hopefully, Jordan had been equally as lucky.

Chapter Twenty-Five

E llie felt like she needed to be several people at once at this moment. Take care of Kate, who had slumped over in the corner of the room, crying hard. At least, hospital security had arrived, and she could safely call for backup, then get a stinking murderer out of the patient's sight.

Slowly, the threads started to unravel.

A young nurse accompanied Kate out of the room. When their eyes met, Ellie nodded to her friend. She'd be safe.

A few minutes later, Casey walked into the room, shaking her head at the angry drug lord with the stain at his crotch. "My, Harding, you have a way of scaring people. Let's get this gentleman to the station, where he can have a long talk with Carpenter and Henderson when they're back."

"Have you heard anything at all about Jordan?" Ellie asked anxiously.

Casey shrugged. "Last thing I heard, backup was on the way."

That wasn't good enough. TJ Pratt was the only missing piece in this complex puzzle, and he made threats early on. Serious or not, Ellie didn't like the idea of Jordan having a run-in with him, her biological father, a ruthless criminal.

She tried Jordan's number again, but the call went to voice-mail.

Jordan shouldn't have been on this case, she thought, but then again, this case had developed so many branches it was almost impossible not to get involved—and Jordan needed to work. That was something Ellie could understand. Casey was silent, probably aware of the thoughts that troubled her.

Once outside, they witnessed a man being rushed into the ER, and another ambulance arriving with a woman clearly in shock, blood on her face and shirt. Kathryn Larson. Behind her, Jordan emerged, looking tired, but otherwise unharmed.

Ellie halted, and for a long moment, she just stood and stared, barely trusting her eyes.

"Go," Casey said after Ryder was safely locked into the back of the police car. "Don't take too long though. He's not going anywhere, but neither is that stink." His glare would have almost been amusing if Ellie had taken the time to care.

She caught up with Jordan in the waiting area.

"Hey. Jordan, wait." Instead of asking all the questions that were on her mind, she simply embraced her. Jordan held on tight in return, letting go only reluctantly after a while.

"I know you need to go," she said with regret.

"I'll be back as soon as I can," Ellie promised. "We busted Ryder here tonight, not long ago actually, Kate and I..."

"Good job," Jordan said, sounding tired.

"What about Pratt? Is he..."

"They don't know yet."

"Oh. Okay." Ellie was trying to figure out what to say, but her cell phone rang, a text from Casey that said *Now would be good*.

"I'm sorry. I'll come back. My partner's got a bit of a sensitive nose."

She could tell from Jordan's expression that she didn't get the joke, but that didn't matter now. They were both okay, or, at least, would be—together. That was all that mattered to Ellie.

Chapter
Twenty-Six

K athryn didn't seem to be physically harmed, but Jordan wasn't willing to leave anything to chance. She sat in the waiting room after Ellie was gone, replaying the disturbing family reunion in her mind. She'd had no choice but to shoot Pratt, blood spattering all over the terrified woman next to him. Those were the cards she'd been dealt, genetically speaking, a brutal criminal who might or might not live through the night, and a frightened woman who spent the better part of her life trying to escape from it, with drugs and sex.

Jordan shook her head tiredly. She couldn't afford to believe in genetic determinism, or she'd be screwed.

The only reason she was still waiting here was to tie up loose ends, of the case, of her life. It didn't mean all that much.

"Detective Carpenter?"

She flinched at the doctor's soft-spoken address.

"You can see your mother now. She'll be fine, but we'd like to keep her overnight for observation."

"I'm not...She's..." Jordan realized it would take much longer to explain the situation, and that the doctor probably didn't have the time or inclination to listen to all of it. "All right."

Over the years, it had been impossible to ignore the evidence. Jordan knew she'd been lucky to escape the life she'd been heading for in the company of Kathryn and Jim, who would never change their ways, not for themselves, certainly not for a child. If anything was wrong with that, well, then it had to be somebody else's fault.

Still, when she stepped into the room, Jordan was struck to realize the woman in the hospital bed wasn't at all what she remembered. Even in the past few days, from the first time she'd seen her at the department, she looked older, more fragile. Of course, her lifestyle wasn't favorable to aging well.

"I guess you heard," she said. "They'll release you tomorrow."

"They better. I don't have the money. Jordan...Could you sit down for a moment?"

Hesitantly, Jordan did. Just tonight, she reminded herself. She had to wrap up this case.

"He came to threaten you, because of Serena?"

"I always knew he was a bit crazy, but I couldn't believe...until now..." She shuddered. "You saved my life."

"That's my job. He would have killed both of us if he'd had the chance. I suppose you underestimated him all this time."

Kathryn gave her a sad smile, but Jordan wasn't willing to let go of all the anger and disappointment of decades in a matter of moments. *How could you?* she wanted to say. Granted, getting pregnant and married right out of high school, the beginning of a rapid slide down the social ladder, had to be hard. Jordan couldn't remember Kathryn making the attempt, ever, to get out. Jim Larson might have been incapable or unwilling to provide for his family, but he hadn't been abusive or pressured her to stay in any way. They had simply given up, both of them, and having Child Protective Services do the job for them was the easiest way out of the responsibility.

"Okay." She got to her feet. "I'll send a detective to get your statement tomorrow."

"Wait. Please. I need to know something."

Jordan had the inappropriate impulse to laugh at her. *You think I have answers for you? Think again.*

"You came to help me. Don't you think that means something?"

"It means I didn't want you to die. I haven't changed my mind on having coffee."

Kathryn nodded. "Maybe someday you will. Maybe someday, you'll be able to see my point of view and...We thought we did what was best for you, give you the chance at a better life."

"You didn't give me that chance. CPS, and Jack and Pauline did. It doesn't matter now."

"It does matter," Kathryn insisted. "All I want is for you to give me a chance."

"With all due respect, Ma'am, I believe that's not up to you to decide."

Jordan spun around to see Ellie standing in the doorway. "I need to speak to Detective Carpenter," she said.

"And who are you?" Kathryn asked, her bitter impatient tone much more reminiscent of the woman Jordan had once known.

"I'll bring you some clothes tomorrow. Try to get some sleep," she said and followed Ellie out of the room. Jordan was grateful for her presence and, at the same time, self-conscious about it.

"I didn't think you were going to come back."

"I snuck away," Ellie confessed. "Everyone's busy with the big bust tonight, although technically the big deal was Ryder pissing his pants. Before you ask, I didn't make him do it, I guess that was Kate, but it was...interesting, in any case. Darla Pierson is going to be okay."

"Thank you."

"That's only the abbreviated version. I'm sure Derek will be able to tell you more about what went down at Ryder's house. I'm so glad you're okay." Her voice got a bit shaky on the last words.

"Same here. What a day. I meant to thank you for arriving when you did."

"She doesn't have the right to ask anything of you. You risked your life to save hers."

Split-seconds. Jordan thought that she would have to go through the motions again, like the last time when she had to fire her gun and shoot a perpetrator ready to kill first—in less than nine months. It was getting old. At least, both Darby and Pratt were alive, for now. If Pratt made it through the night, he'd be likely to get a life sentence for the numerous deaths he caused, for what? There was never a real reason, just greed and power play.

"I'll bring her the clothes. That'll be the last of it, and I swear, it only gets better from here. I can't wait for you to meet Jack and Pauline."

"I can't wait either," Ellie said, her smile warm and affectionate, reminding Jordan that in spite of all the detours and incidents, something was going right in her life. It gave her an idea.

The pieces were coming together. Apparently, Hobbs had been boasting about his connections with major drug suppliers when still in prison. Pratt thought they might be helpful and thus made a deal with Ryder whose primary goal it was to get back at Mara Lyman, the woman who had dared to leave him.

That sort of entitlement was tiring at best, but in this case, it had cost too many lives.

Jonathan Darby had felt entitled, too, punishing women who, in his deranged perception, led an immoral life.

Jordan wasn't thinking of Darby when she climbed the stairs to Mrs. Clayburn's apartment. It was early, but she had hoped to see the elderly woman before returning to the hospital.

Mrs. Clayburn let her in, her expression somber.

"I wanted to let you know we caught the man who murdered Mara," Jordan said. "He wanted to set her up, too, but we learned the truth."

"She didn't do anything wrong, did she?" Mrs. Clayburn asked, tears in her clear blue eyes.

"No, she didn't."

Jordan wasn't the only one who had risked her life to save others. She was going to make some calls on Darla's behalf, but first she had to make sure Kathryn had something other than the hospital gown to wear when Derek was finished with her statement.

"I made some tea," the elderly woman said with a hopeful tone to her voice. "Would you like some?"

Jordan was about to decline, but she decided she could spare a few minutes. After some tea and cookies and conversation with Mrs. Clayburn, she left to get Kathryn some clothes.

Ellie was waiting for her at the trailer like she had promised. No, Jordan remembered, she had asked to come, and Jordan had decided she had to stop assuming everyone would treat this situation as something to trap her, material to use in a bitter argument.

Not Ellie.

If she was serious about letting her know what she was getting herself into, Jordan owed it to her to open the door this much. It wasn't a big space to begin with, so it didn't take her long to locate a set of underwear and socks, pants, and a shirt. Funny how memory worked as a warning system. The feeling of being trapped and about to suffocate came easily, but it was hard to tell whether that was remembrance of her childhood, or the hours spent in Darby's basement.

There would be another case, and another after that, and eventually, they wouldn't all hit so damn close to home.

Jordan nearly dropped the bag she was holding. She hadn't even meant to open the last drawer of the cheap old dresser about to fall apart, and see the open tin box, a handful of photographs—of herself, as a baby, a toddler, then a pre-school child. The timeline was torn off abruptly after that. In spite of the visual proof, she had hardly any connection, any memory of that time. She had always thought Jim and Kathryn hadn't kept anything of hers, intent to cross her out of their lives like she had done with them.

What a cruel joke.

"Jordan? Are you okay?" Ellie came closer hesitantly.

"No, damn it." If she wanted to be honest, she might as well start by telling the truth. Very little had been okay in too long. She wasn't ready to have coffee with Kathryn yet.

"You'll do what feels right," Ellie said, brushing her hand down Jordan's back. "That's the most important thing, what feels right to you. They owe you answers, but you'll ask them when you're ready."

"I'm not sure I'll ever want to know."

"If you don't, that's fine, but remember that little girl was strong enough to make it through the worst of it. That is what matters." Ellie was crying. "I know who you are...and I love you."

This was probably not the right moment to ask her if she'd ever considered having children, but right here in this place that was still a crime scene, Jordan wanted to believe that they could make it and do better—as a couple. Maybe, one day, as parents.

"I love you too," she said.

For the first time in a long time, those words felt real.

Chapter Twenty-Seven

"I can't believe that after everything, you're still nervous about meeting the parents. I wasn't kidding when I said it gets better," Jordan told her, amused. "They're good people."

"I don't doubt that. They raised you, after all. You're sure this will do?" Ellie asked with regard to the lilac-colored dress. She'd been wearing it when she arrived at Jordan's house. Currently, she wasn't wearing anything, and they were about to be late because of Jordan's attempt at relaxing her.

"It's just dinner. As long as you wear something, it'll be okay."

"Funny," Ellie muttered, but Jordan's hands on her naked body soon distracted her from any worries about the first impression she'd make on the Carpenters. She sighed, helpless to the pleasure of fingertips wandering up her thigh and between her legs.

"You're relaxed enough now?" Jordan asked, kissing her neck gently, the caress sending a shiver down her spine.

"Not anymore..."

"I'm sorry about that, but we're going to be really late if we don't leave soon..."

"It's okay. Let's do this." Ellie reached for her dress and put it on for the second time this evening. Truth be told, she was curious too.

It was a good thing that Jack and Pauline Carpenter didn't live far away, and so they made it—decently dressed and without further incident—in under half an hour.

Ellie stayed at a respectful distance when the couple embraced Jordan.

"You must be Ellie," Pauline said, shaking her hand. "I'm so glad we finally get to meet you."

"Me too. Thanks for having me." Ellie was sure she had to be bright red, and she could tell from Jordan's small smile that she'd noticed it too.

"Come on in," Jack said. "Dinner is ready, but we can sit down and have a glass of wine first."

They sat in the den, and for a moment, Ellie was overcome with emotion as she realized how meaningful this scene really was, for her, for Jordan. These were people who hadn't hesitated to step up to the task. They had the means to help a child in a bad situation, so that's what they did.

She knew so much more than she had when first aware of her attraction to Jordan, but Ellie had never been more certain that she wanted to be here, with her. It felt good to be certain of something.

After dinner, Jordan offered to make some coffee, and Ellie followed her into the spacious kitchen, happy, and the tiniest bit tipsy—she'd been nervous after all, drinking that red wine a little too fast. "This is going well," she said. "They're good people, like you said. They're not going to ask you about anything you're not ready to talk about." Damn, now was not the moment to cry again.

"I know." Jordan kissed her softly. "I needed to stall for a bit after...everything, but I'm glad we came here. There's something I wanted to tell you, but there was no time earlier. It's all good," she added quickly, when the alarm must have shown on Ellie's face. "Everyone's been telling me I should have taken more time off. You know how it is—the first day of work can't come soon enough."

Ellie nodded.

"Everything that happened...It put some things into perspective too. We try to do as much as we can, but there comes a time..." She laughed, a bit nervous. "What I'm trying to say here is that I decided to take that vacation no one could get me to take, after all, and I want you to come with me. I hope you won't be mad at me. I talked to Bristol, and he said it would be fine. A week from now, we could be on the beach and be lazy for a while, until we get bored."

"That is...Wow. Yes. I mean, no, why would I be mad?"

"Because I booked us two weeks all inclusive? I know I should have asked you, but I wanted to surprise you. It's..."

"Magical," Pauline finished the sentence for her, a happy smile on her face. "Ellie, I hope I'm not out of line when I say you're very special to make that happen. I can't remember the last time Jordan had a real vacation, and I'm pretty sure she can't either. If there was ever a good moment, I'd think this is it."

Between the lines, Ellie could easily read the emotions, the worry and fear of the past few months, and she understood. They didn't need to know everything that happened in Darby's basement, but they did need to know that Jordan would be okay. She'd do her best to help with that. There was no doubt she could use a vacation herself.

"When do we go?" she asked, making both Jordan and Pauline laugh.

They decided to let the night wind down at the *Code 7* later, retreating to a table in a corner after they'd said hi to a few of their friends. Kate and Casey sat at the bar with Derek Henderson, Libby and Wes at another table.

So many memories in this place, Ellie reflected, sad, bittersweet, hopeful…and that one time she and Jordan had hid in the bathroom, because they had nowhere else to go. That particular memory made her face flush. They were lucky they could just go home and pick up where they'd left off earlier. No more hiding, no more secrets. If the past few months had taught them anything, it was that their lives were better when they were together—and so much more satisfying.

Ellie even felt generous to spare a brief thought for Bethany and wish her well. If they could pick up the pieces and start a new life, so could she.

The text message came in when Jordan had left for a moment to talk to Detective Doss.

I wish I could be with you tonight.

Ellie thought ruefully that this was one small inconsequential secret she'd have to keep, at least for a few days. Soon, they would be sipping cocktails under palm trees—before that, she'd get a new cell phone after all. She didn't want anything to spoil this new beginning.

Chapter
Twenty-Eight

E ven with her suitcase packed and in the trunk, and a key to the house left at Derek's, Jordan could hardly believe this was going to happen, two weeks with Ellie away from all responsibilities, just lazy days on the beach. Well, probably they'd still spend a substantial time indoors, based on the past few days.

Being happy could be a dangerous thing, a lot more than settling for a less than satisfying situation—with the latter, you didn't have that much to lose. Maybe that's what Bethany had liked, not having that much to lose. There was no turning back now, not that Jordan wanted to. She had cut ties where needed, and maybe, one day, she might find Kathryn and talk to her, like two adults, and find closure. That part wasn't so scary anymore, since it sank in that the choice was up to her.

Jonathan Darby thought he was so special, but in the long run, he'd be nothing but a fading nightmare. He had lost. She was living proof to that, just like Judy Lawrence and Lori Gleason.

Jordan was still unsettled about the fact they'd never found out who sent the messages to Ellie, but either way, she had given

Darby too much credit. He wanted to play a game, but that would be hard to do if no one else was playing.

Ellie wasn't waiting on the sidewalk when she parked in front of the apartment building. Jordan couldn't help smiling. She had overslept which wasn't a surprise after all the long nights not entirely due to work.

The door stood ajar, so Jordan slipped inside and climbed the two flights of stairs to the apartment—no need to wake the neighbors taking the elevator at this time of night. They still had plenty of time, almost three hours until boarding.

At Ellie's front door, she rang the bell and waited. No sound from within the apartment. She punched in the numbers of Ellie's home number. The phone rang, but no one picked up. Ellie's cell phone was turned off.

When Jordan tried the knob, the door opened, confirming...Something was wrong.

"Ellie?" She stepped into the dark apartment, almost stumbling over the suitcase right by the door. Ellie's coat hung on the rack, but her purse was gone.

No answer.

The bed looked like it had been slept in, no visual sign of disturbance in the bedroom or bathroom, or anywhere in the apartment—but the door had been unlocked. Ellie wouldn't run out without locking behind herself. She had no relatives in town. There was only one more person Jordan could think of that might need Ellie in the middle of the night. As unlikely as this scenario was, it would be so much better than any of the alternatives.

A missed flight wouldn't be the end of the world—it was just money.

When she dialed the number of the division, Libby Marshall answered.

"Kate? She's here with me. Is everything all right? Aren't you supposed to be on vacation?"

A moment later, Kate McCarthy was on the phone, sounding distressed. "What is this about? I didn't call Ellie or vice versa. I thought she was with you."

The darkness was overpowering for a moment, enveloping her, making her speechless. Ellie hadn't run out because one of her friends needed her.

"I'm at her apartment. McCarthy, I need you to drop whatever it is you're doing and come over here."

She heard the shocked gasp at the other end. "What are you saying? What's going on?"

"I don't know yet. All I know is she's not here, and with you and Marshall being accounted for, there's no explanation." Jordan didn't want despair creeping into her tone and her mind, not so soon, but she couldn't help it.

It wasn't fair. This couldn't be happening, to Ellie, to her.

She took her time searching the apartment more thoroughly, trying to trace Ellie's steps from when she'd last seen her.

Just a few hours, Ellie had said, to pack, make sure everything was turned off in the apartment, and sleep until two in the morning.

Her alarm was set and had gone off correctly.

Where was she?

Jordan went back to the front door, taking a closer look at the lock. It didn't seem like it had been tampered with in any way—if anyone other than Ellie had come in, they must have had a key, or she let them in.

In the middle of the night, the night she was supposed to go on a vacation?

Not likely. Turning off the light in the hallway, Jordan bent to regard the lock from the other side, when the small line on the outside of the door, just above the floor, made her stop.

There was blood, not much of it, but the sight made her heart skip a beat anyway. She sank to her knees, brushing her hand over the dark red carpet. Her fingers came away wet.

She made the call in a calm and collected manner, refusing to think of the worst just yet.

We will have those days in the sun, I promise you.

I will find you.

About the Author

B arbara Winkes writes sapphic crime drama and Christ-
mas romance. She loves writing characters who get the
job done, whether it's stopping a predator or saving cherished
traditions—while still making time for love. She lives with her
wife in Quebec City.

barbarawinkes.com

Also by Barbara Winkes

The Crossing Lines Trilogy
Undercover
Redemption
Vengeance

The Connected Series
Promised to the Queen
Drawn to the Enemy
Tempted by the Protector